THE C

Now she was free of all her obligations, Jessie could come home, to the woods she had always known were waiting for her. For a year she was free to paint the animals she loved. Only first, there was Michael Haveron to contend with . . .

Books you will enjoy
by MELINDA CROSS

LION OF DARKNESS

There was no physical reason for Cassie's continued blindness. But Wyatt, the man who helped many blind people to cope with real life, found that he was not able to help Cassie, for their impact on each other got in the way of his help . . .

WHAT'S RIGHT

For Ruth Lyons and Tray Hampton, loving one another seemed so right. As if they had always loved, even before they had ever met, and that now was the fulfilment of a timeless promise. But there was Tray's duty to Christie and the life he had ruined—no matter how right he and Ruth were together there could be no betrayal—no deceit.

THE CALL OF HOME

BY

MELINDA CROSS

MILLS & BOON LIMITED
15–16 BROOK'S MEWS
LONDON W1A 1DR

First published in Great Britain 1986
by Mills & Boon Limited

This edition 1986

ISBN 0 263 75488 X

Set in Monophoto Times 10 on 10 pt.
01–1086 – 60648

Typeset in Great Britain by
Richard Clay (The Chaucer Press) Ltd,
Bungay, Suffolk
Printed and bound in Great Britain
by Collins, Glasgow

CHAPTER ONE

THE train wheels knocked in a steady, monotonous rhythm, measuring the miles in tiny jolts which she found strangely comforting. Get-a-way, get-a-way, get-a-way, they said; and as long as she heard them, felt them through her body, she was content. But when the train stopped, as it had often on the long, cross-country trek, her slender body tensed with impatience, relaxing only when the wheels started grinding slowly forward once again. For Jessie Loren, the need to keep moving was almost obsessive.

She sighed and pressed back deeper into her seat, savouring the silence of the almost deserted car. There would be no more stops now until the last one, and she was totally relaxed.

The long, low wail of the train's whistle made her jerk upright in her seat and frown into the darkness outside her window. After a moment of tense watchfulness, she settled back again. Just a crossing, she comforted herself. Don't worry. It won't stop again. That was just a warning blast for some sleepy town's railroad crossing. Her small, perfectly formed mouth curved in a smile that was almost smug. You're almost home free, she thought. Home, and free—up-and-coming main attractions—two things you haven't had for almost twenty years.

She let her gaze drift until it fastened on the reflected face that stared back at her from the darkened window. She was coming to know that face at last, and it was one of the things she had marvelled at on this long, cross-country trip. She was twenty-eight years old, and never until she boarded this train had she taken the time to study her own features. But then, she'd never had the luxury of so much time before.

Large brown eyes appraised her coolly, reflectively, as if she bore no relation to the image she was examining in the dusty, smeared pane of glass. She saw something different in the face now; something that had not been there before. It was almost as if this ride were an excursion back in time, and every mile that passed beneath the train's wheels subtracted a moment from her own age as she thundered on towards her childhood home. You're getting younger, Jessie, she said to herself. By the time you finally arrive, you'll probably be eight years old again—exactly the age you were when you left.

She had been right to choose the train, as if she had known in advance that she was travelling to meet her destiny, and that such trips should be prolonged and relished. Besides, there would have been no sense of distance in a three-hour plane ride, no sense of change; and Jessie desperately needed to feel both.

She had watched the landscape alter gradually from her window all the way from California. It had been a strange sensation, watching the background transformed behind her reflection, as if she were testing her face in all sorts of surroundings to see where it fitted in. Certainly not in Los Angeles, even if it had been her home for the last twenty years. She had been smothered by the smog, the waste, the futile, childish, mobile rush of the city. Even miles away she had imagined thick, dirty fingers of heavy air snaking out all the way to the mountains, trying to pull her back. She had felt cleaner somehow in the cradle of the Rockies, then had tingled with contained exhilaration when the train began its endless plummet down the eastern grade of the craggy peaks. She felt safer on this side of the mountains, shielded from the responsibilities that had held her captive on the other side; but still it wasn't right. The flat, arid sameness of the desert had stretched into infinity, and her face looked tiny and lost with the long stretches of baked sand whizzing by behind it. Lost, too, in the golden waves of plains wheat, ready for harvest, and in the black, industrial smoke of Chicago. It was only lately, with the wild north woods of Michigan's upper peninsula streaming by behind it, that the small, serious face had started to look as if it belonged.

She stretched luxuriously, fingers and toes tingling with the prolonged lack of motion. Short arms, she thought, eyeing the brief expanse of chambray shirt extended before her. And short legs, stretched to their full length, with well-worn moccasins barely reaching the empty seat opposite. No wonder California had spat her out after twenty years of trying to swallow her. She had been outlandishly alien in that land of tall, golden bodies with sun-bleached hair. Her own was long, straight, and such a uniform brown that it hardly looked like hair at all, more like a silk curtain with no highlights and no texture. Besides that, her delicate complexion freckled horribly in the sun; and her constant earnest expression, totally devoid of humour, had no place among the permanently fixed smiles of the natives. The carefree, sun-loving, fun-loving populace of the California beaches had always found something a bit odd about Jessie Loren; and more than one relationship had ended with the pronouncement that she was just too serious, that she didn't know how to have fun. But life was a serious business, and Jessie often thought of Californians as delightfully innocent but slightly irresponsible children. She didn't belong there. She never had.

But will you ever fit in anywhere, Jessie? Can you really carve a space for yourself in this world, find people you can relate to? The nagging doubts prodded relentlessly at her thoughts, and she squirmed in her seat as if that would rub them out. She forced herself to close her eyes and listen to the music of the wheels. They were still talking, still comforting her with that easy, gentle cadence which kept time with her heartbeat; only now their message had changed. It wasn't 'get-a-way, get-a-way, get-a-way' any more. Now it was 'yes-I-can, yes-I-can, yes-I-can'. When she realised what chant was running through her mind, she opened her eyes and smiled. Yes-you-can what, Jessie Loren? Yes-I-can anything, she answered herself immediately. Just like always.

She awakened hours later to the pale, sickly light of a timid dawn filtering through her window. She squinted at the brightness, immediately aware of the intense quiet of a stopped train.

She straightened quickly in her seat, wincing at the cramps of stiff muscles, and craned her neck to look back the length of the car. An old conductor ambled up the aisle towards her, wearing a smile so broad that it was almost foolish.

'Good morning, Missy. Was beginning to think I'd have to shake you awake.'

'Sorry,' she mumbled, trying to shake the sleep out of her head. 'Have we been stopped long?'

'Just pulled in a few minutes ago.' He jerked his head towards the window. 'And there it is in all its glory. Potter, Michigan. The end of the line, and your stop, I think.'

She turned her face to the glass and peered out at the old wooden station, squatting in the mist of early morning, looking like something carved out of her memory. 'Look at that,' she whispered. 'It hasn't changed a bit. Looks like it crawled out of the last century.'

'It did,' the old man chuckled, pulling her hand luaggage from the upper rack. 'Potter never changes. Nothing much does, this far north. You've been here before, then?'

Jessie nodded absently, still staring out of the window, caught in that peculiar place where time seems to stop in memory, and intervening years fall away.

'Your baggage will be unloaded in a minute, Missy; but there's still no one here. You got someone to pick you up?'

Someone to take care of you, she thought. That's

what he really meant. Her slight build, her diminutive stature, her delicate, childlike features—all combined to prompt an almost universal protective instinct in every man she had ever met. It had amused her once, but now it only irritated her.

'No,' she said firmly as she rose and faced him. 'But I know where I'm going, and I'll find a way to get there.'

The words sounded abrupt, almost pretentious, and she regretted them immediately. 'It's nice of you to be concerned, though,' she added quickly, forcing a strained little smile.

He helped her off the train, then stood next to her awkwardly, shifting his weight back and forth from one foot to the other, obviously reluctant to leave her there alone.

'It'll be all right,' she reassured him with a smile, and finally, doubtfully, he stepped back up on to the metal steps.

She stood alone on the worn planks of the broad platform, surrounded by the untidy heaps of a year's worth of luggage.

One year, she thought anxiously. You've got one year to make it, then the money runs out, and back you go. 'Good luck, Jessie Loren,' she whispered aloud. 'I wish you very good luck.' Then she pulled the tangy scent of pine deep into her lungs, and experienced the first bittersweet pang of homecoming.

It was foolish, she knew, to sense homecoming for a place she hadn't seen since she was eight; a place without family or friends or any of the things that were supposed to be dear and familiar. Yet there it was. She was home at last, and every fibre of her being knew it. She turned slowly to survey her surroundings.

The station itself was an oddity, set in the only open space in the great stands of towering white pine. It looked as if someone had made an awful mistake, planting this peculiar symmetrical structure in the midst of the haphazard grace of a primeval forest; for the trees completely concealed the town from view, and the station house was the only man-made structure in sight. Only the train hinted that civilisation still existed somewhere, and now the train was pulling away. The whistle sounded twice as she turned to watch the woods swallow the caboose, and she felt like an old friend was leaving her behind, calling out a last, mournful farewell. The whistle sounded once more from a distance that seemed greater than it was, and then there was silence. Silence so deep, so intense, that even the scuff of her shoes on the platform would have seemed an unforgivable breach of the peace. She stood absolutely still, holding her breath, letting the quiet seep down to her soul.

'Good morning.'

She jumped and spun at the sound of a human voice behind her.

'Hey,' a big man chuckled, climbing up the platform steps. 'Didn't mean to scare you. You look like a doe I caught by surprise once—big-eyed and ready to fly.' He thumped across the planks towards her, one huge hand outstretched, a broad, white grin slashing the dark blond of his full beard. 'Name's Toby. Toby Christian.'

She stared at him suspiciously, one brow arched in cautious appraisal.

He cocked his head, frowned a little, then looked at his hand hanging foolishly in mid-air. There was nothing quite as defeated as an unshaken hand. 'I may be the resident giant,' he said seriously, 'but I'm totally harmless. Believe me. I saw the train stopping longer than usual, and figured somebody might be needing a ride.'

She gave in to a thin smile and let her hand slip into his hesitantly, surprised as she always was by the extreme gentleness common to very large men. 'Sorry,' she said. 'I'm still suffering from a big-city distrust of strangers. Ny name's Jessie Loren, and don't tell me you're the local cabbie. You look too much like a lumberjack to be anything else.'

'Logger,' he corrected her, grinning. 'Don't ever say lumberjack up here. You'll be an outsider forever. And there isn't a cab in Potter. Not much call for one until hunting season starts, then Zeke Samuels sits here in that godawful hearse of his waiting for the hunters to pour out of the train. But that's weeks away yet, and you don't look much like a hunter anyway.'

'Good. Next to a Californian, a hunter is the last thing I'd want to look like.' Her words were crisp, delivered with a no-nonsense slap to the consonants which sounded like a door slamming shut.

'And what do Californians look like?'

She pursed her lips in thought, then replied flatly, 'Like very tall children.'

His brows lifted in mild surprise. 'I take it you're from California, and it isn't the promised land after all.'

'I'm from here, actually,' she said, lifting her head to take in the tops of the ancient trees, 'but it was a very long time ago.' She dropped her gaze and drilled him with it, assessing him expertly, instantly, and deciding in his favour. 'But I do need a ride, and I could use a hand with all of this.' She waved at the stacks of baggage. 'Are you for hire?'

He shook his head strongly, catching the morning sun in the lighter strands of his hair. 'We only charge tourists up here, and from the looks of that stack, you're going to be here too long to be a tourist. That means you'll be a neighbour, and for neighbours there's never a charge for a helping hand. Where to?' He snatched the heaviest of her bags with an apparent lack of effort, and made his way round the station house to where a four-wheel-drive pick-up was parked.

'The Loren Resort,' she answered, gathering up as much as she could carry and hurrying behind.

'Can't say I ever heard of it.'

She dropped her load at the back of the truck and frowned. 'That's impossible. It's the biggest resort on the peninsula, and it's only a few miles from here.'

He lifted the bags easily into the back of the pick-up,

frowning, then suddenly his face cleared. 'You must mean the Haveron place. I heard it used to be a resort, years ago. Big lodge up near Route Nine; a few cabins?'

'That's it. Right on Loren Lake.'

He shook his head and grinned. 'Loren. Of course. I should have recognised the name. So your family used to run that place...' He sobered quickly and turned towards her. 'You're going to stay at Haveron's?' The question was almost an accusation.

'Good Lord, no. I don't even know them. Mom kept an acre of land and one of the guest cabins when she sold the place five years ago. I'm going to live there for a year.'

Toby was strangely silent, looking down at her speculatively from a height which his heavy work-boots made even more intimidating.

She knew what he was thinking. She must look like a toy to a man well over six feet; a helpless woman barely capable of taking care of herself, let alone spending a year alone in a wilderness cabin. She saw the veil of protective instinct in his eyes and swallowed her indignation, reminding herself that she was now in a part of the country where men were still the great white hunters who took care of women like her. At least he had the good sense not to voice his doubts.

'Well,' he sighed, turning back to the platform. 'It'll be interesting, anyway. Go on. Climb in. I'll grab the rest of your things.'

CHAPTER TWO

SHE marvelled at how much she remembered of the small logging town as they drove down Potter's one and only street. 'It all looks the same,' she murmured, staring out of the window. 'It's like going back in time.'

'How far back?' he asked, eyes fastened on the road.

'Oh my. A lifetime. We left here when I was eight—almost twenty years ago.'

She turned sideways on the seat to face him, noting the classic profile all but hidden by the bushy beard. They'd eat you up in California, Toby, she thought. One look at that rugged face, that lumberjack body, and the beach girls would drop like flies at your feet.

He turned and smiled at her scrutiny with the easy confidence of a man who is used to admiring glances from women. 'Why did your family leave? Wasn't the resort making money?'

There was something odd in the tone of his voice, as if he already knew all the answers, and asking the questions was only a test.

'As far as I know the resort was very profitable,' she answered quietly. 'It was a hunter's paradise then, and we were booked solid every year. But when my father was killed in a hunting accident, Mom simply couldn't handle the place on her own. Couldn't even stand to be there without Dad.'

He seemed deep in thought, his eyes narrowed and fixed on the road as if he were weighing words before he spoke them aloud. 'You might find things a little . . . different here now,' he said finally, and she frowned at the note of caution in his voice.

'This look familiar?' he asked a few minutes later, turning the truck off the main highway on to a narrow lane through the trees.

'No. Are you sure this is it? I remember the road being much wider. Doesn't look like anyone's used this trail for years.'

'No one has, except Haveron, and even he doesn't use it much.'

'Haveron? Just one?'

'The one and only.'

'I don't understand. If he bought the resort. . .'

'It may have been a resort when you lived here, Jessie; but now it's just an enormous piece of very, very private property.'

She squinted out of the windscreen as the truck laboured up the bumpy trail. Underbrush nearly obscured the faint tracks through the grass, and more than once she wondered if they hadn't missed the road altogether. Then suddenly the guest cabin appeared through the trees on the left, and she caught her breath at the ache of memory. 'There it is,' she whispered. 'Right there. First cabin this side of the ridge.'

Toby guided the truck through the maze of trunks and pulled to a stop next to the log structure. 'Looks more like a full-fledged house than a cabin,' he remarked doubtfully.

"It is! It is! Come on!' She could barely contain her excitement as she clambered out of the truck and rushed to the narrow front porch, reaching out to touch the hand-hewn pillars as if they were old friends. She paused there, looking down the slope to the only open meadow for miles around, and let childhood memories wash over her. Suddenly the excitement left her face, replaced by a dark, hard expression that pulled Toby up short when he stopped beside her. The childhood had been too short, she thought bitterly. It had ended far too soon.

'Something wrong?' he asked quietly.

She took a deep breath and tilted her head to look up at him. 'No. Not a thing. It's all just as I remembered it.'

'From the look on your face I'd say they were some pretty black memories.'

She stared at him reflectively. He really was a tremendously attractive man; undeniably virile in all respects except for that eager, boyish expression which marked a man whose life had been easy. She hated that look with the galling envy of one who will never be able to wear it. What would he know of black memories with that open, affable face? That naïve, blind trust which he wore like a badge? This was the face of a man who believed all the tired clichés about tomorrows, and second chances, and maybe even rainbows. Just like her mother. She resented him suddenly, and could barely contain her hostility. 'We all have some black memories,' she said coldly, shutting him out.

One side of his mouth curled slightly, and he leaned back against the post, crossing his arms over his massive chest. 'Why do I feel like someone just slammed a door in my face?' he asked quietly.

She stared up at him intently for a moment, then dropped her eyes and sighed. 'I do that,' she said softly. 'I seem to do that all the time.'

He remained motionless for a long time, then straightened and brushed his hands on the front of his jeans. 'Why don't you open the place up?' he said. 'I'll start bringing in your things.'

She watched his broad back move away, down the steps, towards the truck, shaking her head sadly. He was right, of course. She had slammed a door in his face. She always did that—whenever anyone threatened to become a friend; when they were too attractive, too appealing, too perceptive—that was when she closed them out. Attachments were very dangerous things. They weakened you, like her mother's dependence on her father; and then, when fate took them away, it left you floundering and helpless. And if you were a strong person, as Jessie was, they obligated you; just as she had been obliged to care for her mother for the past twenty years. Love, friendship, all those touted emotions which sprang up between two human beings—they were suffoating, binding ties that gripped you in a stranglehold that never let go. It was easier in the long run to avoid them altogether.

She blinked once slowly, then turned towards the door. Toby had already deposited all her baggage on the porch before she managed to force the rusty lock to yield. He stood behind her in respectful silence as she pushed the door open on protesting hinges.

'Well,' she said, peering inside. 'Looks like I have my work cut out for me, doesn't it?'

'Oh, I don't know,' he mused, seeing through the layers of dust to the possibilities underneath. 'A little spit and polish will do wonders. As a matter of fact, it's one of the nicest places I've seen up here.'

An enormous fieldstone fireplace dominated one wall of the living-room that ran the full length of the cabin. A small kitchen could be seen through a doorway leading to the back, where a bedroom and bath were tucked out of sight.

'This must have been some place,' Toby murmured, making the room seem small as he moved his bulk around it. He lifted one of the dust covers and exposed the chair underneath. 'You lived here when you were a kid?'

'Not here. In the main lodge, just over the ridge.'

He nodded once, and when she made no further attempt at conversation he moved back towards the doorway, leaning one large hand against the frame. 'Haveron lives there now. In the lodge.'

'Does he?' she asked without interest.

'He's not what you'd call . . . neighbourly. I'd steer clear of him if I were you.'

She smiled perfunctorily. 'You make him sound almost sinister.'

He chuckled without humour. 'He is that, as I'm sure you'll find out before too long. He'll go through the roof when he finds out his sanctuary's been violated.' He slapped the doorframe with a resounding crack that made her jump. 'Well, I have to be off. Anything you need before I go?'

'No, wait just a minute.' She reached for her purse and started digging through it. 'I'd like to pay you for all your help . . .'

He shook his head in exasperation. 'Like I said before, there's no charge for neighbours.'

'But . . .'

'And I'll be offended if you offer again. They tell me in town I'm too big a man to offend.'

He stood framed by the doorway's light, trying to look gruff, but he looked so much like an overgrown, mobile teddy bear that she had to smile. 'You are indeed,' she said, liking him in spite of herself, but liking people too much was a risky business, and she quashed the feeling almost instantly.

His lips lifted in a slow, easy smile, as if he had read her thoughts. 'By the way,' he asked, 'do you have power out here yet?'

'I should,' she answered, moving towards the wall switch. 'I called ahead to have it turned on.' She flicked the switch, and there was a satisfying glimmer through the dusty shade of an old standard lamp. 'Let there be light,' she said, smiling up at him.

He stook a sudden step backward, as if he had seen something startling in her face.

'Anything wrong?' she asked.

'Nothing,' he said dully, then shook his head as if to clear it. 'Nothing at all. It's just . . . that you're a very pretty woman. I hadn't really noticed it before, until you smiled like that.' He shrugged helplessly and grinned, then turned and walked away without another word.

She moved to the doorway and stood there, following him with her eyes, almost numbed by the compliment. Her brows twitched in an uncertain frown, and her thoughts fluttered between indignation and astonishment. It wasn't that she was unattractive; she knew perfectly well that her features were delicate and arranged pleasantly on the tiny heart-shaped face; but they were rigid, too, with a forbidding, closed aspect that had prompted more than one man to describe her as 'hard'. No one had ever seen beneath the veneer to grasp at an adjective as soft as 'pretty' before.

Pretty. She wasn't sure she liked it, and her frown deepened. Pretty women were vulnerable and dependent, like her mother, leaning on others with a crushing weight far out of proportion to their fragile frames. They sapped the strength of the strong people who loved them, and left brittle, empty shells in their wake.

She had a brief, vivid mental image of her mother as she was years before, sitting glassy-eyed in a shabby rocker, curled in on herself while a miniature Jessie struggled to make contact. And even then, locked away from reality, beyond Jessie's reach, she had been a very pretty woman.

Pretty, and weak, her mind lashed out with a bitterness that astounded her, and she pushed the memory back where it belonged.

Toby was standing by the truck, watching her carefully. She forced a false smile and lifted one hand in farewell. 'Thanks again, Toby!' she called out to him, and he nodded and waved from the truck before he pulled away.

She went back into the cabin and stared at her baggage thoughtfully, troubled a little by the encounter with Toby Christian. He was like a hundred other men she'd met in California, yet not like them at all. The bronzed, blonde California looks were deceptive, for he wasn't nearly so shallow. Right in the middle of one of those high, exuberant expressions of his, his eyes would suddenly go still and thoughtful, as they had when she'd turned on the light. Living up here must do that, she decided. It must make a man occasionally aware of the seriousness of life. There were no games in the north woods, no second chances. You learned to play by nature's rules, and nature played in deadly earnest. The weak and the frivolous were weeded out in a hurry.

She shrugged Toby out of her mind, and heaved a great sigh at the disorder around her. Then she tore into the stacks of luggage, searching for one particular crate. She paused when she found it, running her fingers along the edge, feeling the familiar quiver of anticipation. She slit the tape carefully with the small pocket-knife she always carried, then laid the familiar articles out on the dusty floorboards. Canvas, stretcher boards, paints, brushes, pastels . . . life itself. The sum of what Jessie Loren was, what she ever could be, lay there before her like a disjointed collection of puzzle pieces, waiting for the magic to make them a unified whole.

'And now it begins,' she said sonorously; then laughed aloud at her own sense of melodrama.

CHAPTER THREE

It had been harder than she thought to find the old glen. It wasn't that the landmarks had changed so drastically—the creek was still meandering through the same stand of birch; the cluster of rocks still dammed the mouth, just as they always had—but everything looked slightly different through eyes that were twenty years older than when she had seen it last. 'The forest changes constantly,' she remembered her father saying, 'yet it remains forever unchanged.'

When she finally broke from the heavy cover of trees and started down the gentle slope that ringed the pond, nostalgia squeezed at her heart, and she was once again that eight-year-old girl, trying to sneak up on the deer. There were no animals drinking now, of course. She had been far too clumsy, too noisy coming through the underbrush, and the forest creatures would have been forewarned. But she'd learn it again, she promised herself. Learn to move silently through the woods, as much a part of the forest as its own. She was just out of practice.

She settled on the slope with her back against a tree, the sketchbook propped on her knees. It was strangely disorientating to find herself in this particular place again; and amazing to find it so unchanged. The great white trunk of the dead elm still bridged the pond; the cat-tails still swayed in the morning breeze; and the soft mud at the water's edge still boasted a myriad of footprints, silent testimony to all the creatures who watered here.

This had been her place, her special, private place away from the clamour of lodge and people; that place which her eight-year-old mind had presumed was reserved for her alone, among all the world's people. This was what she had missed all those years, what she had crossed the country to find; the feeling which consumed her now, cradling her in the warm security of knowing that she belonged. After so many years of feeling displaced, Jessie was finally home.

She took a deep breath, selected a pencil from the case in her shirt pocket, and held it suspended over the blank page, trying for just one moment to resist the force that moved her. But whatever it was within her that transformed life to art took hold quickly, moved the hand that held the pencil, and Jessie Loren ceased to exist. She was no longer a woman sitting quietly on a wooded hill, sketching a scene. She became the scene, and the drawing, as if part of her resided in each realm, and that magical flow from eye to hand merely pulled the two parts together. She became totally absorbed by the process, oblivious to the sounds and smells around her; and so it was that the voice, when it came, startled her terribly.

'What the hell are you doing here?'

Her hand jerked uncontrollably, dragging an ugly black pencil line across the drawing. In that split second of magnified awareness everyone feels when frightened suddenly, Jessie heard the frantic pounding of her own heart, even as her muscles contracted to spin her round.

'Dammit!' she shrieked without thinking. 'You scared me half to death!' And after this verbal release of her fear's first adrenalin rush, she let the image of the man record on her consciousness.

She had never seen such rage on a face before—not quite like that—bold, glaring, and ugly. The memory of a school play popped ludicrously into her mind, where all the children had acted the parts representing emotions. Happiness, Sorrow, Fear, Rage. Little Tommy Meister had screwed his chubby face into a fearsome mask of anger, and, frightening as it had seemed at the time, it was no match for this. This was the real thing: grown-up, adult, naked rage. It was impossible to see beyond it to the man. Even staring right at him, she had no idea what he looked like.

She hated the instinctive fear that coiled in her stomach like a stone serpent; hated this man for causing it; and within seconds the hate overpowered the fear. 'Who do you think you are?' she demanded hotly, eyes flashing in a face now coloured bright red. 'You have absolutely no right sneaking up on me like that! And look what you've done!' She flung her sketchbook to the ground, gesturing wildly, then jumped to her feet and spun to face him.

Glaring up into those eyes was like glaring into a mirror, and the experience struck her hard, rocking her backwards a step. Not that they looked alike; even without taking a detailed inventory of his features she knew that. But the expression was the same—the same one she would catch unexpectedly on her own face whenever she caught a glimpse of her reflection. Later she would realise it was that slightly haunted look of anyone who stands completely alone.

She had surprised him a little, maybe by the surge of her own anger, or maybe because he saw the same thing in her face that she saw in his. Whatever the cause, she saw the rage seep slowly from his expression, as if it had only been the temporal fury of a wave crashing on the beach, then falling back, totally spent.

He stood rigidly erect, towering above her in a posture of quivering threat, but he made no move towards her. 'You're on my land,' he said simply, distinctly, as if he expected her to have difficulty understanding the English language. He had spoken quietly, with none of the sharpness that had marked his first sentence; yet she had the unshakable impression that the voice had come over a public address system, with those deep, tonal echoes which seem to vibrate at the base of your spine. It was a beautiful voice, a magnificent voice, one that belonged on the stage, or in the clouds, or anywhere but standing here in the middle of nowhere, used by a man who was mere mortal, after all. Just hearing it was an intense physical sensation that left her numb with surprise, standing there foolishly with her lips parted and her eyes wide. It was the voice of the forest, she thought fancifully. If the forest could speak, that was what it would sound like.

He frowned at her silent, rapt attention, obviously uncertain of what to do next. 'You're on my land,' he repeated, and her parted lips formed a smile, totally against her will.

'Oh,' she said foolishly, still staring at him, still caught in the spell of that voice.

The sharp call of a jay overhead startled her to attention, and she blinked several times in confusion, like someone waking from a long sleep.

'Oh,' she repeated, regaining her composure. 'Then you must be Haveron, the resident ogre.'

He narrowed his eyes slightly and declared, 'I am,' and she felt the power of those two words all the way down to her toes.

She took a deep breath to steady herself, brushed her hand against her hip, and extended it stiffly. 'I'm Jessie Loren, your neighbour.'

'My *what*?' he roared, and she jumped backwards in surprise, jerking her hand to her side.

'Your neighbour,' she responded carefully, watching him with a wariness born of a deep instinct for survival. 'I own the first guest cabin, the one furthest from the lodge. I moved in this morning.'

'You moved in?' The voice was different now, uncertain, laced with disbelief.

'That's right,' she said defensively. 'I'll be living there, for a year at least.'

He made no reaction whatsoever to her statement, which she thought, from this man, might be the greatest reaction of all. For the moment he simply stared down at her, fixing her with a gaze that made her feel like a bug pinned to a board.

She was transfixed by the stare, as she had been a moment before by his expression of rage. Instinct kept her gaze locked on his, and it occurred to her in the intervening silence that she was absorbing this man's presence in stages: first the voice, now the eyes.

They were set at a slight slant, embellishing the expression of hostile suspicion which she suspected was an integral part of his character; and for all their vibrant green colouring they were flat, revealing nothing, and strangely forbidding. She had seen eyes like that staring back at her from many a canvas, for they were very like those of the wild animals she painted. Compassion would never cloud this man's reason, she realised; or love, or spiritualism, or any of the other distinctly human emotions. He was above all these, or sadly beyond them; for those were the eyes of an animal whose decisions are instinctive more than thoughtful, and that was what made him dangerous. There was no humanity in him.

He blinked once, regarding her with a profound lack of interest which she found more disconcerting than contempt. 'Loren,' he said finally. 'The little girl.'

He knew her, then, or at least knew of her.

'That's right. My family owned this place once. All of it.'

'I'm well aware of that.' He shifted his gaze then to look out over the pond, negating her presence by ignoring it; and for the first time in her life Jessie wished she were privy to the thoughts of another human being.

Freed from the stare that had focused her total attention on his eyes, she relaxed a little and examined the man as a whole.

In her years-long love affair with art, she had never once encountered a person whose presence moved her to paint. Her only inspiration had been the clean, honest, intensely passionate scenes of nature. Wildlife, landscapes, these were the things worthy of oil and brush—never man, with all his murky, complex deceptions glinting from eyes that plotted and calculated, or, worse yet, reflected an empty non-caring that chilled her soul. But this man, this stranger with the incredible voice and the straightforward, almost merciless eyes of a wild animal, this man nearly drove her to the canvas. It was all she could do to keep from scrambling for her sketchbook; and for the very first time a fear of inadequacy trembled deep within her. Could she ever capture the essence of such a man, and render it two-dimensional?

His body was slender, tensed for motion even at rest; and she knew instinctively that when it moved it would be swift, graceful, and above all silent. Like her own, his hair was uniformly coloured, but much darker, wavering so perilously between black and browns of all shades that it was difficult to categorise. It was cut badly, hanging over his forehead in a wanton sheet, curling darkly over the collar of the deep-green flannel shirt.

And the face—it was simply extraordinary. She had never seen one quite like it. Not handsome, at least not in the traditional sense of the word; for the features were too angular, too sharp to be considered easy to look at. Yet there was an absolute invincibility about it; a quiet, supreme assurance that was disturbing and fascinating all at the same time. The skin was oddly unlined, as if the face had never been used to demonstrate emotion; yet the overall impression was one of great age, or perhaps great experience, far beyond the thirty years or so she guessed he must have lived. She would have paid to see that face had it been a work of art hanging in a gallery, and in a strange way she felt that she was doing just that. She had the uncanny feeloing that simply looking at this man was a very expensive test, and that few would see what she saw.

His head lifted slightly and his nostrils flared, as if he had caught a strange scent on the wind. His posture, the steadiness of his eyes, his entire presence suggested a oneness with the forest around him that made her suddenly feel like an intruder—as if he belonged here and she didn't—in this one place on earth she had claimed as her own long before this man ever laid eyes on it.

'When I was little, this was my special place,' she said

suddenly, defensively, as if she were arguing her right to be there. Without realising it, she had placed tight little fists on her hips in the posture of a child, willing to fight with paper broadswords to defend her piece of ground.

He took note of her stance, saw it for what it was, and humiliated her with a short, derisive laugh that sent a chill shivering down her spine. His complexion was very dark, from sun, heritage, or a combination of both; and had the laugh contained any mirth at all, the startling contrast of white teeth against dark skin would have been striking. As it was, the laugh was cold with the contempt of one who finds very little amusing, and it made her more defensive still.

'What's so funny?' she demanded.

He sobered almost immediately, and when he spoke his voice was flat. 'You're particularly possessive about a piece of property that no longer belongs to you,' he said. 'If I remember correctly, your family retained—against my wishes, I might add—one acre, and one acre only with that cabin. You're far beyond the boundaries of that acre now, and as such you're a common trespasser.'

Even forewarned by Toby, Haveron's words surprised her. She hadn't expected an open-arms welcome, but she hadn't expected such seething hostility either. For the briefest of moments, Jessie found herself envying those leggy, blonde beach-goddesses in California. It was hard to imagine women who looked like that being treated as coldly as Haveron was treating her. The moment the thought crossed her mind, she pushed it back, hating herself for the weakness that made it occur to her. So, she asked herself, if you possessed feminine allure, would you play on it? Use it the way so many other women do, to get what they want from men?

She bent from the waist to retrieve her sketchbook, snapping the cover shut as she straightened. His eyes were flat and watchful when she focused on them again.

'Look, Mr Haveron,' she began steadily. 'I have no

intention of violating your privacy or your land. As a matter of fact, I came back here for a little privacy of my own. But we're stuck with each other as neighbours, like it or not, and I'd appreciate the simple courtesy of your permission to enjoy the woods. Is that asking so much?'

He never even stopped to consider his answer. 'Yes, it is.'

'What?' she breathed, unable to conceal her astonishment. After all, she'd asked him nicely, very nicely, for the simple privilege of walking his land. How could he possibly deny such a harmless request?

She forced a winning smile over clenched teeth and opened one palm in persuasive supplication. 'I don't think you understood me, Mr Haveron. I'm not asking for permission to farm timber, burn the forest, or slaughter the wildlife. I'm an artist. I only want to explore quietly, to paint, to appreciate. I wouldn't be bothering anyone, or anything, for that matter.'

He was so much taller that when he looked down at her his eyes seemed to close halfway in an expression of total disdain. 'I understood you perfectly, Miss Loren,' he said coldly. 'And the answer is still no. No one walks my land, for any reason, except me. No one. There are no exceptions.'

Dammit, if it hadn't been for that outrageously marvellous voice, trilling along the sensitive pathways of her nerves even as the words it spoke infuriated her, she could have shrieked at him, slapped away that loathsome expression of control; maybe even battered him with her sketchbook. Instead she simply stood there, quivering with anger, trying to keep her voice from trembling, totally unaware that her eyes revealed all those emotions anyway.

'You are the most unreasonable man I've ever met,' she said slowly, 'and if you think I'm going to mark my acre and stay chastely within its bounds for the next year, you're mistaken.' She thought she detected a glimmer of a hard smile touching his mouth, but with that face she wasn't about to bet on it.

'I take it you don't believe in the concept of private property, then,' he said smoothly.

'Of course I do!' she exploded, stamping one tiny foot for emphasis.

'And yet you don't seem to respect the rights of the property owner. Now how do you explain that?'

It was a smile. It really was. Turning up the corners of a mouth she would have thought etched in stone; but the eyes weren't smiling. They were still and expressionless, making the curve of his mouth oddly menacing.

She took a deep breath and blew it out through puffed cheeks. 'I do believe in private property,' she said finally, 'and in all the rights that go with it. But I also believe in courtesy between human beings, in granting simple favours that mean a great deal to someone else, especially when it doesn't cost you a thing.'

He regarded her with mild interest, saying nothing, and she thought perhaps he might relent.

'Besides,' she continued, somewhat encouraged, 'I've always thought of this particular place as mine, with the rest of the forest belonging to everyone. No one can really own the woods. It belongs to itself, more than any one man.'

He spoke very softly, and his eyes never wavered. 'Then you're the one who's mistaken, Miss Loren; because I own this forest—or at least 749 acres of it—and I protect my ownership with whatever means become necessary. If you think you can trespass without consequences, I suggest you ask in town what happened to the last person who entertained that notion.'

He was gone before she could even take note of his leaving, like a wild animal who melts so quickly and silently into its surroundings that one wonders if it has ever been there at all.

She stared blankly at the spot where he had been, wondering what she would do with all that anger and frustration, now that the focus was lost. She let the satisfying rage of impotence build to the point of fantasy, and thought all the way back to the cabin of a dozen things she could have said, if they'd only occurred to her at the time.

CHAPTER FOUR

'HELLO, Mr Ellis,' she greeted the proprietor of Potter's general store gently, as if the spoken word would be enough to blow the fragile-looking elderly man away.

He raised a head crowned with wisps of white from the ledger he was examining, and smiled past the pipe stem clenched in his teeth. 'Well, I'll be damned,' he said quietly, shaking his head for so long that it seemed like a motion he was helpless to stop, once it had begun. 'Jessie Loren, as I live and breathe.'

She nearly laughed out loud at the tired old phrase. 'Don't tell me you recognise me, Mr Ellis. I must have changed a little since I was eight, although I must admit you look exactly the same.'

'I was so old when you left that it was impossible for me to look much older,' he chuckled. 'And my, yes! You've changed. But you look so much like your own sweet ma did then, I'd know you anywhere. Besides, Matt from the power station let us all know you were coming home. Good news it was, too. This town surely missed the Lorens. It's nice to have one of you back, at least.'

It was easier to give in, to accept the offered chair pulled up to the old pot-bellied stove than it would have been to try a polite refusal. Before she'd uttered one sentence in answer to what she'd been doing for the last twenty years, the little circle of chairs was filled with faces she recognised from her childhood, and a few new ones. She hadn't been surrounded by a circle of people so interested in her since she'd left Potter as a child, and she was surprised to find herself literally basking in the warmth of reserved friendship these conservative northerners made obvious without a word. It was as if the chair she now sat in had been empty all these years, waiting for her. These people never forgot friends and neighbours. They just saved your place.

'How is your Ma, Jessie?' Mr Ellis prodded her. 'Did she . . . come around all right?'

She winced at the tactful reference to her mother's emotional state after her father's death. 'She isn't a strong woman, Mr Ellis,' she said, choosing her words carefully, phrasing her thoughts in the terminology these men would understand. 'But then, you'd know that. She never was. Depended on Pa for everything. Without him, the world just never seemed right to her.'

Mr Ellis nodded in understanding, then poked a tall, gangly young man next to him and said in an aside, 'You're too young to remember, Wallace, but Jessie here lost her pa some years back in a hunting accident.' He shook his head and clucked his tongue against his teeth. 'Terrible thing. Tragic. Didn't know that Mizz Loren would ever recover, she was so set back; and poor Jessie here just a little wisp of a thing when it happened.' He jerked his head to the side as if to shake away the memory of a bad time, then returned his attention to Jessie. 'How was it in California, Jessie? You lived with your ma's sister, didn't you?'

Jessie leaned back in the chair with a pained smile. 'For a while. Then we found a place of our own.'

'Well?' he urged her. 'How was it?'

Her smile turned grim. 'Hard,' she said flatly. 'But we managed. We got by."

Twenty years flashed through her mind with the speed of thought, and she seemed to shrink in the chair, remembering. She could feel the beginnings of a bitter laugh crawling up her throat, clamouring for release, and swallowed reflexively. Is that what you call it? she asked herself silently. Getting by? When the tables turn and the daughter becomes the mother, when you manage the finances and care for the house and cook the meals and feed a silent woman with a spoon for years on end, is that what you call it? Getting by?

'It took a long time,' she said steadily, holding the

raging memories inside, 'but Mom is fine now. Remarried, in fact, just this year.' She smiled genuinely, thinking of Walt, standing next to her mother at the station, as fiercely protective as the devoted hound he so comically resembled. She had kissed his sagging cheek in a blind rush of affection, passing on the torch of her mother's care to that man who took it so willingly. He would be a good husband, a stalwart shield between the gentle woman and the world that baffled her so. Where had he been, she wondered, all those years since her father's death when she had been the only buffer? All those years when she had watched her childhood slip away? He must have read her thoughts in that moment, for he said, 'Go be young now, Jess. It's time.' And then she had climbed on to the train and started to live as old obligations became tiny, distant specks the wheels left behind.

'Well now, that's just fine!' Mr Ellis's exclamation snapped her out of the past. 'That was a woman who needed a man if ever I saw one. An old-fashioned woman. Don't see many of those any more.' Then he looked straight at Jessie and the sharp old eyes seemed to peel away the layers to say everything, without saying very much at all. 'It must have seemed like a long time coming for you, young lady.'

She nodded slowly, almost mesmerised by the uncanny certainty that this old man knew everything that had happened to her over the last twenty years.

'Well,' he said, slapping his knee, breaking the spell, 'Potter sure hasn't been the same without the resort. We sure felt the loss.' Every head round the circle moved up and down sadly. 'Economy went to hell without the income from the hunters. Oh, we still get some, but not nearly what the resort used to bring in. Most of the businesses closed up years ago. Me and Hattie's Diner—that's about all that's left.'

'And that Haveron scares away most of the hunters that would come up to hunt on other property.' Jessie recognised Don Peltier, as swarthily complexioned as his French father, and from all appearances just as stubborn. 'Everyone's afraid they'll get lost in the woods and step over his property line accidentally, and end up like Bart Masters.'

'Who's Bart Masters?' she asked.

'A no-account poacher, if the truth be told,' Mr Ellis put in. 'Hunted on Haveron's property just for spite, and out of season, too. None of us was really sorry to see him get what was coming to him, but it didn't do much for the tourist trade, that's for sure.'

'Did Haveron catch him and call the sheriff?'

Ellis cackled in high amusement, and the rest of the men joined in. 'He caught him all right, but he didn't call the sheriff. No, sir. Shot him, right on the spot.'

Jessie's eyes widened as she remembered her earlier encounter, and Haveron's warning to ask in town what happened to the last trespasser on his land. 'Shot him!' she exclaimed. 'And then what? Why wasn't he arrested? Put in jail?'

'Shoulda been!' Elmer Harton burst in, but Mr Ellis held up both hands and shook his head.

'Not so, Elmer, and you know it. Masters should have gone to jail if anybody did, much as we'd all like to see Haveron out of here.' He leaned over his bony knees towards Jessie. 'Seems Masters took a shot at Haveron first, when Haveron threatened to take him in. Wasn't much else he could have done but to shoot back. And it was only a foot, after all,' he reminded the circle of men. 'Haveron could just as well have killed him, if he'd been a mind to.'

The words made Jessie shiver. 'I met him this afternoon,' she said softly. 'Haveron.'

'Oh boy,' said Peltier. 'I'll bet he was madder than a rabid wolf to find someone living at his front door. What'd he say?'

She made a small face and shrugged. 'He told me I was trespassing, and said I should ask in town about what happened to the last trespasser.'

Don stood so quickly that his chair fell over

backwards. 'Now that's going too far!' he roared. 'Threatening a pretty young thing like this. I tell you, it's time we did something about that man!'

Jessie recoiled instinctively at being called a 'pretty young thing', hating the label for all the helplessness it implied. She smiled wryly, wondering what these would-be protectors would think if they knew what a tough old bird this pretty young thing had grown up to be. 'Do you work for the logging company, Mr Peltier?' she asked, just to change the subject.

He blushed to be asked a direct question, retrieved his chair quickly and sat down with a hard thump. 'Not much else to do up here, ma'am,' he muttered shyly. 'Always wanted to be a guide when I was a kid. Used to think then I might work for your pa when I got old enough.' He sighed deeply. 'But there aren't many hunters that come up here any more, so I'm stuck as a logger. And it's not much of a living, I'll tell you. Not fit for a woodsman.'

He spat out the last words bitterly, and Jessie felt her heart go out to these men who had seen their livelihood and lives changed so drastically, simply because a piece of property had changed hands. She knew better than to ask why they didn't move away. Some had, of course; but not the men who circled her now. These were the diehards, the true woodsmen, a breed wavering on the edge of extinction, who could no more leave the harsh, unforgiving north woods than they could stop breathing.

'It's too bad the resort didn't sell right away,' she said commiseratingly, 'to someone who would have kept it just as it was.'

Mr Ellis smiled sadly. 'There aren't many who would choose such a life left in this world, Jessie; and the ones that would couldn't afford such a huge hunk of land. To tell you the truth, we were surprised it ever sold at all. This Haveron fellow coming out of nowhere and just snapping it up for cash—well, we just couldn't believe it. That was a fair piece of change, even with the price as low as it was.'

She nodded grimly, thinking of the desperately lean years before the property finally sold. 'Well,' she said, slapping her knees and rising, suddenly uncomfortable in this group of sullen men, 'if you'll fill my order, Mr Ellis, I should be heading back now. I haven't even begun to unpack.'

She was immediately besieged with offers to drive her home, help her get settled, and see her doors all locked safely for the night. She refused with gracious laughter, pointing out of the window at the one thing she had unpacked and assembled: her faithful ten-speed with a bike trailer hooked behind.

Mr Ellis eyed the vehicle with head-shaking scepticism as he packed the groceries in the trailer a short time later. 'Crazy contraption,' he muttered. 'And those skinny tyres won't get you far after the first snow.'

'I've got these,' she smiled, slapping her legs, 'and a sled. It's only two miles to the cabin, and I'll start stocking up now so that I can go longer between trips in the winter.'

'Two miles can be a mighty long way when the winter storms start,' he warned her kindly. 'And in case you've forgotten, we get our share of storms.'

She felt one of those rare smiles which come from deep inside lift her eyes and her lips at the same time. 'I've been waiting twenty years to see another Michigan snowstorm,' she confided. 'To tell you the truth, I'm looking forward to winter.'

'Make sure you've got plenty of wood!' he called after her as she pedalled away. 'That electric heat won't do much good with all the power lines down!'

But the wind in her ears blocked out his last words, and she waved in answer to what she assumed was simply a cheery farewell.

Funny, she thought as she felt the first strain on her legs a mile later. Not one of those men asked me what I was doing here, why I had come back, how I earned my living, or any of the things most people would be eager to know. But these aren't most people, she reminded herself. These men are from a different age; an age when occupation and motivation were things you learned about gradually over a period of time—not the first question out of your mouth at a cocktail party. She had always hated the superficial familiarity bred in the city; that unspoken understanding which made every person think they had a right to know everything about someone else, simply because they had lunch together or bumped into one another on the street. She savoured this rare encounter with respect for privacy, until she took more careful note of her surroundings, and realised how very much privacy she now had.

'It's culture shock,' she thought aloud, suddenly uncomfortable to be the only living creature on the deserted stretch of tar.

The narrow black ribbon of road curved smoothly away into the trees, and if she stared without blinking at that point where it rounded a bend and disappeared, she felt as if she was biking into the silence of one of her own paintings.

'You just have to get used to it again, that's all,' she told herself nervously. 'Remember, the last time you rode this bike you were dodging traffic a block away from the noisiest freeway in the world. It's only natural that this should seem a little odd at first.'

When she realised she was talking to herself, she stopped abruptly; but then the silence seemed to close in on her, as did the monstrous white pines. It was a trick of perspective that made it seem as if they were leaning towards one another across the road, blocking out the light with malicious intent. She laughed a weak little laugh at her own discomfort. She who had never been afraid in the squalling, throbbing, very real dangers of city streets at night was distinctly, undeniably nervous on a deserted woodland road. She laughed again, but the sound rang false and mocked the relief she felt when she finally turned into the narrow trail that led to the cabin.

She hadn't realised how fast, how frantically she'd

been pedalling until she topped the rise next to the cabin and nearly ran Haveron down.

She squeezed hard on both brake levers and turned sharply off the trail to avoid him, dumping bike, trailer and herself in the process.

She glared up furiously from her inglorious seat on crackling dry pine needles, thinking in the midst of her anger that he could at least have the decency to look concerned.

'What kind of a juvenile trick was that?' she demanded as she struggled to extricate herself from under the bike.

'Juvenile?' His dark brows lifted slightly, but the rest of his face was expressionless. 'You're racing through the woods on a bike like a madwoman, and call the man you nearly ran down the juvenile?'

'You were just standing there!' she spat out, feeling her face colour. 'Just out of sight, waiting for me to come over the hill! You must have heard me coming, and you could have stepped off to one side; but you just stood there, directly in my path, no doubt hoping I would crash! I suppose you're terribly disappointed that I didn't break a leg!'

She took a deep breath after this tirade, hoping that would still the quivering in her knees, but it was so ineffective that she was forced to sink to a kneeling position before her legs collapsed under her. She covered her weakness by pretending to inspect her bike.

'Are you all right?' There was absolutely no concern in his voice, and she hated herself for wanting him to say more, just to continue speaking, indifferent or not, just so that she could hear the deep, rich sound of his voice.

'Of course I'm all right!' she snapped. 'And what would you care if I weren't?'

'Oh, but I would care,' he said, and she forgot her anger and looked up at him, the words had surprised her so much. 'If you collapse here, you'll block the road, for one thing,' he explained drily. 'Besides that, I'd be obliged to send for a doctor, and that would mean even more traffic in a place where I prefer to have none.'

From anyone else, she would have accepted the words as something said half in jest. It appalled her to realise that this man meant every word. She could die here, and his only regret would be the trouble it would cause, the people it would bring to his precious hideaway.

She stared up at him in disbelief, anger completely forgotten in the amazement of observing a person without a trace of human feeling. He returned her gaze with nonchalance, apparently untroubled by her scrutiny.

All her life she had resented the solicitude of men far less able, and usually less strong, than she was. Never had she consciously wished to be the kind of woman men felt they had to care for. And yet now, inexplicably, this strange man, who obviously was incapable of caring for anything, was evoking that age-old, distinctly feminine response. She wanted his concern—she almost craved it—and the desire was so alien, so repellent to her independent nature, that she could only acknowledge its presence for a moment before discarding it with disgust. But for that single moment she looked up at him with an almost fearful reverence.

He was in all respects totaly unlike anyone she had ever met. His voice, his attitude, his very presence was contradictory to everything she had learned to expect from men. She could not picture him on the streets of Los Angeles, or on the streets of any city, for that matter; and she was struck by the fanciful notion that if he were taken from the woods he would cease to exist altogether. He blended into the forest as if he were an integral part of his surroundings, his lean, straight body resembling nothing so much as the trunk of a healthy young tree. His green eyes remained quiet, steady, and almost insufferably cold, like a predator's eyes, indifferently watching the movement of prey, and for as long as their gazes locked on each other that was precisely what she felt like.

A breeze floated by in a delicate whisper, lifting the irregular fringe of dark hair from his forehead like a mother's caress. She felt suddenly that the forest was a feminine entity, touching and marking one of her own, and again she felt like an intruder.

She rose stiffly, pressing against her knees with her hands, deliberately avoiding his eyes. She righted the bike with some difficulty, bracing it with the kickstand while she repacked the fallen groceries back into the trailer. She kept her back to him during the entire procedure, as surprised that he made no offer to help as she would have been if he had. She felt his gaze burning into the back of her neck as she worked, and when she finished she rose quickly and spun to face him, a stinging remark ready on her lips; but the path was empty. She drew in a quick breath of surprise while her eyes darted in both directions looking for him, but it was as if he had never been there.

'Haveron!' she called out in a voice that sounded more desperate than angry; then regretted that she had called to him at all. She felt strangely diminished, almost demeaned, as if they had met in a struggle of some sort, and because she had called his name she had lost the first battle.

CHAPTER FIVE

THAT she could not stop thinking of him infuriated her. She spent the hours before sunset engaged in a vigorous, victorious assault against the dust of twenty years, and even in the midst of polishing windows or scrubbing the bathroom tiles, she would find herself muttering aloud, practising the scalding retorts she would use when she saw him next. Better yet, she would not speak to him at all. She would ignore him completely, pretend he was just another tree in this forest of trees, no more worthy of note than the dust she was now eradicating. After all, this year was her own escape, her desperate grasp for privacy, freedom, and lack of responsibility for others. He was as much an intruder in her sanctuary as she was in his.

Yet as much as she willed it away, the image of his face kept appearing before her. Despicable as he might be, his face was still extraordinary. It hung suspended in her consciousness as she showered away the grime of housecleaning, as she prepared and ate a light supper of canned soup and bread; and when she finally sank into the easy chair that faced the clean, empty fireplace and closed her eyes, she acknowledged the truth. She would not rid herself of that vision until she had captured it on canvas. It was always that way with scenes she was moved to paint. They would linger in her mind in persistent torment until she gave in and let her mind move her hand. As soon as the vision came to life on canvas, her thoughts would be her own once again.

She fought the impulse to paint Haveron, partly because it would be a homage of sorts to a man she found generally loathsome and particularly disturbing, and partly because she was afraid she could never render the man in two dimensions. She sat for a long time facing the non-existent fire, clenching the arm-rests of the chair to keep her hands still. It was an alien sensation, this enforced idleness with hands completely at rest. She raised one in front of her face, spread the well-shaped fingers wide, and smiled ruefully. Odd that such tranquil beauty could come from hands which had so often been tightened into fists of frustration and despair.

The first time she had put paint to canvas, no one had been more amazed than she. 'It's a gift, Jessie,' her mother had murmured reverently. 'A God-given gift. This is what's really inside you. This is the Jessie I know.'

Funny that her mother had been able to see her stern young daughter in those first serene, restful paintings which she'd pulled out of childhood memories of the woods. No one else could. Not even Jessie herself. They had been too unlike their creator.

She could still see that first painting, even now. All she had to do was close her eyes. It had been amateurish, even childish, with muddy colours and deplorable technique; but still, there had been something about it, something alive that stopped the breath and left lips parted with wonder. She'd sold that painting to a gallery owner who had pursed his lips, nodded his head, and offered to display as much as she could produce. 'You can't learn this,' he'd said quietly, jabbing a stubby finger at the landscape. 'This is inside, from the beginning. Keep painting, keep learning, and bring me everything.'

She had worried that her renderings of the Michigan woods would remind her recovering mother of the time she had lost, and destroy her precarious grip on reality. Instead, the paintings had been the first upward step for both of them. The gallery owner had become her mentor, securing commissions, sponsoring her first exhibit, submitting her work to contests that eventually brought moderate fame. He had even arranged the calendar contract that was financing her return home to

Michigan. 'Think of it, Jess!' he had exclaimed the day they signed the contract. 'Advance money to support you for a whole year in the place you want most to be, and all you have to do is deliver twelve paintings by the end of that time. You'll have royalties from the calendar sales, a flat fee when they print duplicates in their magazine, and more commissions than you can handle when the work is seen nationally. What could be better?'

She smiled, remembering that day. The gallery owner had been Walt, and the only thing better than the calendar contract was his announcement that he and her mother intended to marry. That had been the final turn of the key that truly set her free.

She stopped the reverie with an abrupt shake of her head and a sigh of resignation. She would not be able to produce one suitable painting, let alone twelve, until she drew Haveron's face out of her mind. She gathered the tools of her life reluctantly, and settled back into the chair.

As was her custom, she began with the sketchbook propped in her lap, charcoal pencil poised in her hand. The blank page stared up at her, defying her to fill it, then Haveron's face appeared there, and she had only to follow the lines.

Her hand flew over the paper until she had filled page after page with sketches; some full body, some only the face, in dozens of different poses and in detail that surprised her. She had no idea that her mind had recorded his features so precisely until she saw them come to life beneath her hand. Then, without looking at any of them a second time, she flopped the cover of the sketchbook closed, containing the whole of Haveron safely inside. She had locked him away as surely as if she had turned the key on a cell door, and he would not trouble her sleep this first night in her new home.

She awoke to a raucous symphony of sounds outside her bedroom window, wondering what flight of fancy had ever made her think the north woods were silent. She recognised the busy, impatient chattering of squirrels and the noisy conversation of blue jays, but could only wonder at what other forest creatures joined in the din of greeting a new day. She had been away from the woods too long to sort out the separate voices.

Even though her bedroom window faced east, the sun barely peeped through the panes, thwarted by the massive trees that dwarfed the cabin. It will be very dark here on winter mornings, she thought suddenly, and shivered with foreboding. But on this morning splashes of light painted a random pattern on the bedspread, warming her whenever they touched like prodding fingers encouraging her to rise.

She left the snug comfort of the old four-poster reluctantly and padded to the window on bare feet. 'Satisfied?' she asked the view outside her window. 'I'm up now.' Then her eyes focused clearly on the world outside, and she caught her breath, wondering how people justified living in asphalt jungles when there were places in the world like this.

Shade-loving ferns hugged the ground, quivering under the weight of morning dew. Each one of a million perfect droplets captured the timid sun in a tiny, dancing prism of light. The sun seemed to be rising reluctantly, as if it were almost too difficult to climb high enough to top the towers of white pine. Long, dusty golden rays shot through the forest in a pattern of broken symmetry so exquisitely beautiful that it made Jessie think of magic, and fairy dust, and other things she had not thought of in nearly twenty years.

She would paint this for Walt and her mother, she decided. One morning she would rise early and plant her easel here, right by the window, and capture the magic of a forest morning to send back to the land of palms.

She closed her eyes on the silent promise, then turned away from the scene that was distracting her from what she had come here to do. Business first, she reminded herself. You have twelve paintings to complete for the company before you start painting for fun, and this won't be one of them. It isn't what they want at all.

She had a quick breakfast of canned peaches and toast, then dressed warmly against the chill of a north woods September morning. She chuckled as she pulled on heavy brown corduroy slacks and a matching bulky sweater, imagining how incongruous such garb would be in California's September heat. Putting on lipstick and mascara was such a force of habit that she was halfway through the task before she remembered there would be no one to assess her appearance; no one at all to notice if she did the unthinkable and went out without make-up. It was a new, tiny freedom that made her pause in the motions of brushing her long hair and smile at her reflection. For the space of an instant, with that wistful smile softening her features, she saw someone in the old dresser mirror she had never seen before; perhaps the same person who had promoted Toby to call her pretty.

The eyes were large and deeply brown, heavily fringed with thick, dark lashes. The nose was pleasantly straight and a bit short, perched above a delicately shaped mouth that didn't look at all severe when it curved up like that. It was like turning a corner and coming suddenly upon a stranger who looked vaguely familiar, and the effect made her sober instantly and take a quick step backwards from the mirror. And then, of course, with the eyes narrowing warily at this apparition and the lips tightening into a firm line of tension, the stranger was gone, and the mirror reflected the Jessie Loren she knew.

She nodded with a sort of begrudging satisfaction, pulled another few strokes on the brush until her hair swung in a gleaming curtain round her shoulders, then packed her case and headed once more for the glen.

She settled carefully into the cradle formed by the curving base of an oak's trunk, and began again to sketch the area round the pond. Her strokes were light, her manner preoccupied as she filled in the time with patient silence, waiting for the painting's true subject to appear.

The deer would come, of course. It never even occurred to her that the native wildlife would change their habits over the course of twenty years, and as it happened they hadn't. They still watered at the old pond; descendants, undoubtedly, of the very animals she had watched as a child.

She was just about to shift her weight when the first deer appeared, and as soon as she saw him she knew no others would come until he had drunk his fill and left. If there was any sort of hierarchy in the baffling society of deer, this one must be a king.

At first only the head and neck were visible as he moved from shadow into light and paused to test the air with majestic head lifted, nostrils flaring. Jessie wondered at the weight of his massive rack, easily spreading three feet from tip to tip. Safely upwind, even at this distance she could see the great eyes clearly, examining the glen with liquid indifference. His keenest sense had already scented the air and proclaimed the pond free of danger. He moved with a fluid grace that seemed to defy the mechanics of motion, barely rippling the tall swamp grass as he passed through. His muzzle had hardly kissed the still water before her pencil began flashing across the paper, capturing muscle and sinew, shadow and light of this one position before he should move to another.

She dared not risk the noise of flipping to a new page, so filled her background drawing of the pond with a dozen sketches of this one buck.

She heard nothing; she smelled nothing; yet she was suddenly aware of another presence, even though the deer continued to nibble the moist, tender shoots at the water's edge undisturbed. It wasn't necessarily a sinister presence, but it was in some way she could not define a powerful one, halting her pencil in mid-stroke, demanding that she should turn her head to confront it.

Because she was in perfect control, because not alarming the magnificent buck was uppermost in her mind, she moved her head slowly to look over her left shoulder. Only a slight twitch of her brows communicated her dismay to find Haveron standing silently by the trunk of a nearby tree, his body motionless, his eyes riveted to her drawing.

She was afraid for a moment that he would speak and startle the deer, but although his lips were parted slightly it was apparently just to quiet his breathing, for he said nothing.

He's a hunter, she thought, wise in the ways of stalk and kill, silent and deadly.

He was barely five feet from her, yet she had never heard him approach. Not the slightest crackle of a dried pine needle had betrayed his presence. Something about that made Jessie very uncomfortable. If he had not come so close—close enough to disturb the subtle currents of air round her—she would never have known he was there. A shiver traced a jagged trail up her spine as she realised there would be no privacy, perhaps no safety in the woods with this man. He was too much a part of it. Even now, as she stared at him, his black slacks and turtleneck sweater seemed to merge with the tree trunk he stood by, until it was difficult to tell where the man ended and the tree began.

He had not looked directly at her since she had turned her head, and now, when he lifted his eyes slightly to cover the distance from the drawing in her lap to her face, she felt that he was seeing her for the first time; that up to this point he had hardly been aware of her. She could barely discern the green in his eyes, dark with the shadows of lowered brows, and their expression, if they wore one, was unreadable. The corners of his firm mouth angled ever so slightly, and if it was not quite a smile, it was at least not the rage she had seen on that face yesterday. She was every bit as fascinated by the man as she had been by the buck, and for precisely the same reason. Both were ultimate artistic challenges, compelling her to draw.

He made a quick, impatient movement with his hand, directing her attention back to the deer.

The buck had entered the water up to his knees, so delicately that the still surface of the pond barely rippled. He stood motionless in his own reflection, seeming to grow from it. It was an extraordinary picture, precisely what the company would want for the calendar, and Jessie sketched quickly, almost furiously, trusting her memory to catalogue the nuances of colour that would later bring the drawing to life. For the moment, Haveron was forgotten.

Deer are marvellous subjects, she thought absently as her hand flew across the paper. Unlike all other wildlife, constantly skittering and scurrying about the high-speed business of life, deer struck these majestic, motionless poses and held them for minutes at a time.

Most of her memories of this place—the ones she had transferred to canvas in California in those very first paintings—had in some way involved the deer. They were printed on the circuits of her brain in dozens of indelible freeze frames, epitomising the woods, her childhood, almost life itself. In all the variables of her life, the deer had remained the one symbol of constancy; the single, uncomplicated representation of life in its most beautiful simplicity. Even twenty years had not changed that. She had changed, even the woods had changed subtly, more sinister now with Haveron as a brooding caretaker; but the deer, thank God, were exactly the same.

Haveron. The reminder of him struck the moment the buck turned to stalk elegantly back into the concealment of the trees.

He was squatting next to her, his weight balanced perfectly on the balls of his feet, his arms draped comfortably across his knees. It was a posture of infinite patience, but Jessie knew from experience that the deceptively relaxed position was agony itself for muscles unused to it. She turned her head slowly to look at him, feeling the stiff muscles of her neck protest, wondering how he had managed to move so close without her noticing.

He knew perfectly well she was looking at him. She suspected that very little escaped this man's awareness. Yet he refused to acknowledge her, preferring instead to keep his gaze fastened on her sketches. A fringe of the thick, rich darkness of his hair hung crazily over one brow, but she could see both his eyes clearly, and somehow their expression seemed altered—less two-dimensional than yesterday.

'You're very gifted,' he said quietly, and she responded physically to the rich timbre of the melodious voice, unreasonably clear and distinct after such a long silence.

'Thank you,' she said simply, dismayed to hear her own voice crack weakly. She accepted the compliment as her due, yet was strangely thrilled that it should come from this man, and felt her face flush like a schoolgirl's.

'Has no one told you that before?'

He was speaking softly, she knew he was. So why did his voice reverberate through each and every nerve of her body, leaving her tingling with the same sensation one feels while listening to the mellow tones of a symphony orchestra lingering long after the last note?

'Of course they have,' she remembered to answer, then frowned because her reply had sounded so pompous.

'You blush as if you'd never received a compliment on your art before.'

'I blush easily,' she lied, for she couldn't remember blushing ever before. Not once.

When his eyes finally met hers, directly, intrusively, examining parts of her mind that had never been seen by another human being, let alone a virtual stranger, she experienced two impulses. The first was to lower her eyes. Better yet, to pull a bag over her head to conceal whatever it was he was looking at so intently. The second was to paint his face as it looked at that moment: open, curious, and oddly vulnerable.

She could have done neither, for as long as he continued to look at her she was incapable of motion of any sort. Even blinking required an intense, concentrated effort. She remembered reading of an exotic poison used on the tips of blow darts by some obscure African tribe—a poison that paralysed instantly, rendering its victims helpless. And then she recalled that the venom of one particular snake had the same effect, paralysing prey so that it could be swallowed whole, and alive. That such recollections should be precipitated by the look of one man made her start to shiver uncontrollably, even as her eyes remained helplessly transfixed by his.

He frowned suddenly, and rose to his feet in a fluid motion which broke the spell when her numbed brain recorded the fact that his knees were suddenly where his eyes had been. 'You're cold,' his voice rumbled from above her, and she blinked rapidly, resisting the impulse to look up. Instead she laughed weakly to cover the chattering of her teeth, and rubbed her upper arms briskly with hands that felt numb and useless and larger than life.

'I guess I am.'

'You should bring something to sit on. The gound is always damp here, even on hot days. Come on.'

She risked a glance up at him then, puzzlement touching her finely arched brows. Come on? Come on where? Was he arresting her for trespassing?

The line of his mouth tightened in exasperation as she remained motionless. 'Well, get moving. You should get out of those wet things and sit in front of a fire before you really get chilled. Besides, the rain will start any minute, and it wouldn't do to have this ruined.' He stooped to pick up her sketchbook, closing the cover carefully, then tucked it under his arm.

Her pants *were* wet from sitting on the ground. She hadn't really noticed until he mentioned it, but now the uncomfortable sensation of dampness seemed intolerably cold. She rose stiffly, grimacing at the ache as blood rushed unrestricted down her legs. She stepped tentatively on moccasins squishy with the collection of dew, then glanced up at the sky to confirm his prediction of imminent rain.

'I had no idea it was going to rain,' she said dully. 'It was sunny when I got here.'

'You were busy,' he said, shrugging, and she forgot herself and smiled at him, because he understood that her work made her oblivious to her surroundings. The smile was a catalyst that might as well have been a slap—his reaction would have been just the same. He jerked his head back on his shoulders, his eyes almost disappearing between narrowed lids. Then he turned on his heel and strode away through the trees, leaving her to stumble after on stiff legs, wondering what on earth she had said to offend him.

The first huge drops were splattering on the forest floor by the time they reached the cabin. He pushed open the door without so much as a glance asking permission, and the effrontery startled her so much that she stopped dead on the porch, her mouth open, shivering in the cold wind that was driving in the storm front.

'Well?' he demanded, holding the door wide, gesturing her in as if it were his home and not hers. 'Are you going to stand out there for the duration?'

A sudden gust pushed against her back, and she stepped inside and took possession of the door, as if closing it herself would reaffirm her ownership.

If he noticed her indignation, he ignored it, and walked over to the fireplace with a frown. 'Where's your firewood?' he demanded.

'I haven't had time to bring any in,' she said tiredly. 'I've only been here twenty-four hours.'

Exhaustion had crept up on her with the stealth of a stalking beast, giving no hint of its presence until the first strike. Suddenly she wanted nothing more than for this strange man to leave, so that she could change her clothes, make a hot cup of tea, then crawl under an afghan and doze.

He looked at her quietly for a moment, then, as if he could read her thoughts, he turned for the door. 'Get into something dry and warm,' he said, closing the door behind him as he left.

'And you thought Los Angeles was filled with strange people,' she muttered to herself, thinking of all the abrupt exits this man had made from her presence in the short space of one day.

She heard the front door bang open just as she was pulling off her damp cords, and flung them in a heap on the bedroom floor in irritaton. She should have checked the latch after Havcron left, especially with the wind as strong as it was. She trotted back out to the living-room bare-legged, her long sweater brushing wetly against her thighs, then jerked to a halt.

Haveron had just entered the cabin, his arms burdened with firewood, and was in the process of trying to close the door with one foot. His eyes connected briefly with hers, and even as she stood there, momentarily startled into motionlessness, she thought it odd that his face registered nothing of surprise to see her so scantily clad.

'Are you always this friendly?' he asked drily, and because she was tired and just a little bit punchy, and because the last thing she had expected from this sombre man was humour, she began to laugh. She was still laughing when she turned back towards the bedroom, totally unconcerned that to any man her present state of undress would be tantalising in the very least. Haveron seemed so far removed from the petty temptations which marked the human race that she suspected she could stand before him totally nude, and receive the same, indifferent response.

She was still smiling when she emerged from the bedroom, unquestionably decent in a high-necked navy-blue sweater and jeans. He had coaxed a roaring blaze from the damp wood, and was squatting before the fire, poking at it listlessly with one of the fireplace tools.

'Oh, that's lovely,' she said, kneeling next to him with

her hands stretched out towards the flames. 'It looks exactly like it's supposed to.'

Because he never even turned his head to look at her, she felt perfectly comfortable examining his profile. Some automatic function of her subconscious reminded her that this was one angle she had not sketched, and recorded the image in minute detail. He looked totally different from the side, like another man altogether. Without the indifferent, animal-like intensity of those green eyes staring right at her, he seemed less forbidding, more human than she had thought before. He had a fine, straight nose, high, prominent cheekbones that made her wonder again about his heritage, and a broad forehead, furrowed now in serious contemplation of the fire.

'Trying to place the face?' he asked quietly, still staring into the flames.

She dropped her warmed hands and rubbed them vigorously over her thighs, then curled into a more comfortable position that faced him directly. 'Of course not. Just studying it. It's an interesting face, you know; from an artistic point of view.'

'It should be a familiar one.'

She shook her head with certainty. 'I wouldn't be apt to forget a face like yours. But even if I had,' she added almost involuntarily, 'I'd remember your voice.'

He looked at her for the first time since she had joined him by the fire, a faint line of puzzlement appearing between his brows.

'Never mind,' she said quickly, a little embarrassed to have confessed so much. 'Now why should your face be familiar? Are you famous?'

It was the first time she'd heard him laugh, and the sound was brittle and short, like a crockery plate breaking into two neat halves. 'No, I'm not famous. Nevertheless, you know me. From a long time ago.'

She pursed her lips and thought for a moment, then shook her head again. Her hair swung across her shoulders, catching light from the fire in a smooth, burnished sheen. 'No, I've never known a Haveron.'

'Haveron is my first name. At least it was. Haveron Michels. It suited my purpose to switch them around when I bought this land, so now I'm Michael Haveron.'

She looked up suddenly, her eyes narrowed to peer down the tunnel of her past. 'Michels,' she murmured thoughtfully. 'There was a Michels family who lived near here when I was a child. The mother worked in the lodge sometimes, during the hunting season, and . . .' she turned sharply to look at him, trying to erase twenty years from his features, '. . . and she had a son, but his name was Ron. . .'

'A butchered version of Haveron.'

'Oh.' Without realising it, she had lifted one hand, and now held two fingers thoughtfully against her lips. She frowned as snatches of memory tugged at her mind, looking back at the pictures her child's brain had recorded with adult perception.

He had been a tall, thin, sullen boy, easily six years her senior, and therefore of little but mild, distracted interest to her at the time. And even that had been prompted because he was so odd, so terribly different from all the other children she knew. She remembered too-short pants and bony wrists protruding from the same freshly-laundered, neatly-pressed shirt, day after day, whenever she had seen him. And there had been the thing with animals; the fiercely protective devotion to all wildlife that marked him as weak within a community which depended solely on hunting traffic for its survival. He could not bear to see the suffering of the forest creatues, yet had little regard for any human life. He had been ostracised by his own kind, ridiculed for his poverty, taunted for the wounded animals he treated and then released, and hated for the many times he would chase deer away from some hunter's stand, ruining their chances for a kill.

'I do remember,' she said quietly, blinking to refocus on the present. 'You hated us, because the lodge brought hunters here. I remember my mother telling my father that one night, trying to calm him down. He was terribly angry—you'd destroyed a hunter's stand, and he wanted to fire your mother so that you'd have to move away. But Mom wouldn't let him.'

His face softened slightly. 'Your mother was a very special woman,' he said sternly, as if he didn't want emotions cluttering up his words. 'She was the only truly kind person I ever knew.'

'She still is,' Jessie said softly, thinking how sad it was that the world's kind people were also its weak people.

'She's alive then, and well?' His eyes reflected the first bright, caring interest she had seen.

She nodded slowly. 'She'd be interested to know it was you who bought the land. It was all handled through agents, you know. We never knew who had purchased it, or why. Perhaps you could tell me about it, and I could write to her.'

His expression sharpened, drilling her for a moment with its intensity, then he stood and walked to the window. 'Rain's stopped,' he said tonelessly, 'and I should be going. You'll have to get some firewood in here if you really intend to spend the winter. The power's off more often than not once the snow starts.'

It sounded very much as if he never intended to see her again, and, for reasons she was reluctant to examine too closely, she didn't want him to leave.

'Wait,' she commanded, jumping to her feet. 'There are some things we'll have to get settled before you go.'

He paused by the door, politely attentive, but something in his expression made her feel childish, as if nothing she had to say could possbily hold any interest for him.

'I was trespassing this morning,' she blurted out, and felt even more foolish when his expression remained unchanged.

'I'm aware of that.'

She blushed furiously. 'And I intend to do it again!' Oh God, she moaned inside, fighting the impulse to roll her eyes at her own stupidity.

One side of his mouth turned up in a half-smile. 'Your request for permission is interestingly phrased,' he said wryly. 'I don't think I've ever heard a more eloquent plea.'

'Oh, dammit!' she spurted, angrier with herself than she was with him. 'What do you expect? Asking permission to walk in these woods is like asking permission to breathe! And I intend to continue to do both, with or without your sanction! Besides, I'm not hurting a thing, and I have no intention of sitting up here for twelve months waiting for wildlife to come and pose on my little acre so that I can paint them, and what's more, I don't even know where my acre begins and ends, so even if. . .'

'Enough!' He held up both palms in surrender. 'Do you have rubber boots?'

She released the breath she had been holding and frowned. 'Yes,' she said in confusion.

'Good. Put them on and come along. We'll have lunch at the lodge. You might be interested to see that again. Then I'll show you the places you're most apt to find your subjects. No sense in your tramping all over 750 acres to find what I can show you in minutes.'

She stood immobile as he went outside, her mouth open, her eyes glazed, feeling like a deflated balloon.

'Come on!' he called, and she scrambled for the closet to pull on her boots.

CHAPTER SIX

JESSIE decided she had been crazy to go with him halfway up the narrow trail to the lodge. Haveron hadn't spoken a word since they left her cabin, and she found herself wondering involuntarily if psychopaths were subject to long, brooding silences.

He had obviously slowed his pace to accommodate her own short stride, but seemed otherwise oblivious of her presence. Shouldn't he say something? After all, he'd invited her on this expedition. If he'd intended that they should not communicate at all, he might just as well have gone alone. Unless—her imagination bounded—unless his motives were as dark and sinister as he was.

And he *did* look sinister. In stolen sidelong glances, Jessie noted that he seemed to have taken on the aura of a deathly-still forest after a rain; as if he had no real identity of his own, but was only a reflection of the woods around him.

He moved with absolute silence (stealth, her skittering mind thought), while her own boots crackled constantly on twigs and pine needles underfoot. The sound of only one pair of footsteps created the very disconcerting sensation of walking alone, even though she could see him beside her.

She tried to push down the mounting nervousness which she realised was foolish, but it kept rising up again like a mindless spectre that refused to die.

The trail narrowed as they mounted a small knoll, and the forest seemed to close in around them. Humidity hung in a dreary blanket that scattered tendrils of ground fog like slithering snakes. To either side, gloom beckoned in the rising walls of trees and underbrush.

Say something, she pleaded silently, suddenly desperate that the quiet should be broken, but the only sound was the constant, erratic dripping as moisture slid from sagging pine boughs to splatter on the forest floor.

'Why did you come back here?' he asked suddenly, shattering the quiet and making her jump. She felt like a little bird, helpless in the vice of a human hand, listening to a tiny heart thunder wildly while her startled thoughts scrambled for an answer. He spoke again before she had a chance to reply.

'Never mind. It's none of my business. Well, there's the lodge. Familiar?'

They'd stopped in the centre of the trail, and for the first time she noticed the weatherworn logs of a massive structure peeking through the trees. Her heart twisted in an unexpected onslaught of nostalgia, and she forgot her jumpiness of a moment before, forgot Haveron's presence entirely, and let the memories come.

She uttered a small, involuntary exclamation, then took the lead for the first time; down to the shallow dip in the road that had once seemed steep and treacherous to her tiny child's legs; across the doll-like wooden bridge which spanned a thready creek; up the gentle rise and left into the drive; finally stopping before the broad, welcoming porch that stretched the full length of the building.

'Oh my,' she whispered, climbing the six steps up, remembering how very tall they used to seem. She hesitated at the massive double front doors, then dropped to her knees and ran her fingers along the bottom panel of one. 'It's there,' she murmured as her hand encountered what she sought. 'It's still there.'

Haveron squatted next to her and peered at the worn indentations in the wood that spelled out 'Jessie' in primitive block letters. 'I never noticed that before,' he said quietly.

'You weren't supposed to,' she replied, staring at the carving, moving her fingers over it in a caress. 'It was a secret, between Father and me. Even Mom never knew it was there. You see, I was deathly afraid of bears as a child. Used to have nightmares about them coming into the lodge at night and attacking us while we slept. They were irrational, crazy kid dreams, but nothing stopped them.'

She smiled suddenly, her eyes focused on some point far back in time. 'Then one day Father said if we carved my name on the door the bears wouldn't be able to pass through, even in my dreams. It was supposed to be magic. Even then, I knew it was just nonsense, but it worked. I never had that dream again.'

Haveron rose slowly, and the motion brought her sharply back to the present.

'Sorry,' she murmured, rising herself and looking off into the distance. 'Nostalgia, I guess.'

He had his hand cupped under her chin before she knew what was happening, and the eyes that looked down on her face were strange; almost cloudy with an emotion she couldn't identify. She almost asked him what was wrong, but the feel of his hand under her chin stopped her. It was a peculiar sensation; one that took her back a full twenty years to when her father would cradle her chin in just that way, making her feel cherished and safe. Great, her busy mind raced while her eyes watched his, entranced. Now you're developing a father fixation for this strange man, responding like a child to a gesture that is absolutely meaningless.

But it didn't feel meaningless, and the extraordinary reaction of her body to this man's touch was hardly childish.

'You're an enigma, you know that?' he murmured. 'Tough, self-contained lady. Hard, I think. Very hard.' He shook his head slightly, still fixing her with his eyes. 'And then you talk about your childhood here, or even just think about it, and your face changes, like someone was pulling aside a curtain.'

He dropped his hand abruptly, then turned to the door and pushed it open, his face hard once again, almost forbidding.

She hesitated for a moment, watching him, as his words tumbled over and over in her mind, then he gestured impatiently for her to precede him through the door.

She walked stiffly into the large foyer, nodding with jerky shakes of recognition at things that were painfully familiar. The registration desk, still gleaming with that burnished gloss peculiar to hand-rubbed hardwood, still sporting the ugly gash at the bottom where her tricycle had wounded it a thousand years ago; the wagon-wheel chandelier; the enormous fieldstone fireplace; a few pieces of old furniture, scattered among the newer ones, which jolted memories alive.

She kept walking mindlessly, stopping to look or touch only occasionally, because she knew that if she stopped for long she would have to sit down and cry.

She was eight years old again, roaming the passageways of the huge, rambling structure, loving the old quiet of the off-season when all the rooms were empty and the entire castle was hers. And it was a castle then, she remembered with a wistful smile.

He was talking to her. She'd just been tramping blithely through all the rooms that were his now, without even pausing to ask for permission, and he was following dutifully behind, talking. She wondered what he had said; what she had missed.

'. . . so it didn't take as much work as I anticipated to restore it to its original condition. I have your mother to thank for that, I suppose.'

'What?' She stopped and turned to face him, her expression blank.

'For taking such care when she closed the lodge,' he explained, frowning at her look of puzzlement. 'Draining the pipes, covering the fixtures, and so on. It was almost as if she expected to come back one day.'

A short, mirthless chuckle escaped from Jessie's lips, and her eyes hardened. 'She did,' she said tonelessly, staring through Haveron into the past, not seeing him at all, barely realising that words she had never spoken before were now marching from her mouth with a dull, mindless intention all their own. Her gaze remained fixed, almost glassy, and she spoke in a monotone devoid of emotion. 'She'd calmed down after the funeral—at least, she seemed to. The crying stopped, and her nightmares, and she could converse normally again. Everything seemed fine . . .' Jessie hesitated, her brows twitching slightly in painful recollection, '. . . at least, it seemed fine to everyone else. I never could understand then how she had recovered so quickly when I was still so sad. Until one day . . . and then I started to understand.' She shook her head slowly, back and forth, entranced by a memory that seemed more real than the present. 'She found me crying, you see; and when she asked what was wrong, at first I was surprised that she could even ask that, and then I started crying even harder, and asked her why Father had to die, and how we would live without him. She just stared right through me. She just stared, smiling this strange little smile, and then she told me that I was silly. That we'd go to visit her sister in California for a while, and that when we came back . . . Father would be here, waiting for us.' Jessie shivered as she relived that moment.

'She never said that to anyone else. Only to me. "Don't listen to them, Jessie," she'd tell me. "They want us to believe he isn't coming back, but we know better, don't we? It's our little secret. But we'll have to pretend to believe them."' Jessie's vision wavered, then focused on Haveron with such a wide-eyed, innocent expression that he flinched to see it. 'She was such a quiet, gentle woman, you see,' she continued, 'and she was going quietly, gently insane.' She took a deep breath and let her shoulders sag slightly. 'So we closed the lodge carefully, because she said it had to be ready for us when we all came home.'

When the words finally stopped, Jessie simply stood there, staring straight ahead. The feather-like touch of Haveron's fingers on her cheek brought her sharply aware and she jerked her head to look at him. He was frowning with a tender concern that embarrassed her, because it looked so out of place on his face.

'Ah!' she said, too fast, turning quickly away from his hand. 'Sorry to bore you with all that. I don't know what came over me. This place, I suppose, seeing it all again. I haven't thought about that time in years, and I've certainly never talked about it.'

She was back in total control; a straight-shouldered, straightforward young woman unhampered by the past.

'Come back to the kitchen,' he said quietly. 'We'll have some lunch.'

Within moments she was perched on one of the tall stools that tucked under the huge butcher-block preparation tables, thinking that, although the room seemed smaller to her adult eyes, it was still enormous. Almost every room in the lodge had its own fireplace, but the kitchen's had always been her favourite, perhaps because it was a colourful red brick instead of the customary fieldstone. It covered the entire east wall from floor to ceiling, and the opening was large enough to accommodate the huge swing-arm kettles used occasionally for cooking when winter storms caught them short of gas for the three large stoves.

'It must seem odd rambling around in a place this big,' she mused aloud, 'making a sandwich in a kitchen that used to serve a hundred, having your pick of dozens of beds, sitting alone in a room that seats fifty.'

'No,' he answered quickly. 'It doesn't seem odd at all. In fact, it seems very right. Just as it should be.'

She raised her brows at the strange answer, then shrugged and continued to examine the kitchen. It amazed her to find everything in the large room meticulously clean, and much as she remembered it. The collection of brass pots gleamed from their hangers, although it was doubtful if Haveron ever had occasion to use, let alone clean, the large vessels. The long row of windows over the multiple sinks were bright with recent polishing, welcoming the feeble light that filtered through the damp, dreary forest.

'You've taken beautiful care of the place. It looks as

good as it ever did during the season when we had hired help.'

He smiled perfunctorily as he poured water into the coffee maker. 'You've just come at a good time. I have a cleaning crew in twice a year to put things right. They were here last week.'

'A cleaning crew? From Potter?'

'No,' he said shortly. 'From the outside.' He slammed the heavy door on the huge cold locker and walked towards her with an armload of food packages. 'I'll warm some soup if you make the sandwiches,' he said. 'I'll have the roast beef today, I think.'

She gaped at the incredible amount and variety of food he had stacked before her, wondering why he kept such enormous quantities unfrozen with only one mouth to feed. 'You have a family of twelve locked in a room somewhere?' she asked.

'No,' he chuckled, 'but I had to provide for the crew when they were here. These are leftovers, I'm afraid, and frankly, I'm sick to death of them. I've been eating the same things for the past three days, ever since they left.'

'You must have a large cleaning crew,' she said doubtfully, starting to open the packages. 'Even now, there must be enough here for . . .'

'Twenty,' he contributed, and her brows shot up.

So he has money, she thought to herself. Money enough for the incredible eccentricity of bringing twenty people in from the outside twice a year, just to keep a place that accommodates a hundred people in perfect condition for one. She shook her head almost imperceptibly. Why not live in one of the cabins? Why expend such effort and money to remain in the vast emptiness of the lodge?

When she looked up from her work, he was stirring soup at the smallest of the stoves, watching her warily, waiting for questions he obviously did not want to answer. She stared at his brooding countenance thoughtfully for a moment, then dropped her eyes without a word.

'Didn't your aunt realise your mother needed help when you finally got to California?' he asked without warning.

She frowned at the unexpected question. 'I told you,' she said impatiently, 'she was normal in front of other people. We were already settled in our own apartment by the time she got noticeably worse. And when things got really bad . . .' She shrugged indifferently. 'Well, by that time I could manage.'

'As an eight-year-old?'

'I was nine by then, almost ten, and it wasn't like she was hard to manage. She just sat there, day after day, saying nothing, doing nothing. All I had to do was make sure she ate, and went to bed, and bathed . . .'

'I don't believe it!' he exploded, and a glimmer of the rage she had seen in his face on that first day was back again. 'So a mere child managed the house, meals, took care of an emotionally disturbed woman, and, I presume, went to school as well? Where the hell was the rest of your family? Why didn't they see to it your mother was taken care of properly? And you? Why . . .'

She slammed down the knife she had been using and jumped to her feet, her face livid. 'She *was* taken care of properly!' she shouted. 'If she'd been institutionalised, she might never have got well! And my aunt did help, for as long as she could!'

The sound of her voice echoed in the empty room, haunting her. She sagged back on to the stool, her shoulders straight, her chin up, her eyes blazing.

'So I kept her home,' she said very quietly, fighting to regain control, 'and Aunt Maggie helped until she died.' This last was said so unemotionally that one might have thought Jessie had no feelings for her aunt. Haveron seemed to see through that, for his gaze softened somewhat and he took a deep, calming breath before he spoke.

'And when did your aunt die?'

'When I was thirteen,' she answered tonelessly.

A small measure of exasperation crept back into a

voice he fought to keep steady. 'And you had no other family?'

'None.'

'So from thirteen you were completely on your own?'

'That's right.'

'And where was the great state of California all this time? All those social service agencies that are supposed to step in in situations like that?'

She shrugged casually, her brown eyes as hard as she had ever seen his. 'They didn't know we existed. We didn't need their help. Mom got social security cheques from Father's death, and there was the insurance, and I was working after school by then.'

He stared at her for a long time, then turned back to the stove and dished up the soup. 'I apologise,' he said stiffly, carrying the soup over and sliding on to a stool opposite her.

She raised her eyes briefly and shrugged.

'I had no right to ask any of those questions,' he went on, 'and certainly no right to question your care of your mother. Obviously you did a superlative job, since she's recovered now, and remarried.'

Jessie kept her eyes on the sandwiches she had prepared while she struggled with feelings she didn't understand. She had never discussed those years with anyone, not even Walt; and she couldn't imagine what had prompted her disclosure to a man she barely know.

Haveron took her silence for anger, and continued almost lamely. 'Listen, I do mean it. I am sorry. I've been accused of hating mankind in general, and there may be some truth to that, but when it comes to children . . .'

She looked up at him then, surprised at the uncertainty in his voice.

He continued slowly, drawing the words out in a low, almost menacing whisper. '. . . I simply cannot abide injustice to children. They're the only innocent ones, before adults ruin them. Blameless, just like the creatures in the woods. And yet how they suffer. . .'

His words trailed away into silence, and Jessie felt the beginnings of a smile of discovery starting deep inside.

'Soup's getting cold,' he said gruffly. 'We'd better eat.'

Neither of them spoke during the meal, but Jessie watched him openly, seeing hints in his face of the solemn boy she vaguely remembered. She looked back at what she knew of him with adult compassion, and a sudden understanding of why the pain of children should affect him so deeply. They had been so poor, he and his mother; and he had been lonely even then. She could see that now. He had been the ridiculed outcast, friendless, hurting, cruelly teased because he loved the animals so. The pain of his own childhood was still with him, just as hers was. What had happened to him after she left? What had the rest of his life been like?

'No one here knows who you are, do they?' she asked suddenly. 'You didn't want them to. That's why you changed your name.'

He raised his eyes to look at her thoughtfully, then simply shrugged.

'Is your mother still alive?' she persisted.

'No.'

'Oh. I'm sorry. . .'

'Don't be.'

She closed her mouth on whatever inappropriate remark she had intended to make, then took a deep breath and pushed away her plate.

'Finished?' he asked, and she nodded. 'Good. Then I'll give you the grand tour. Looks like the weather is going to cooperate.'

Jessie lifted her eyes to the windows, and saw golden bars of sunlight piercing the trees. No rainbow, she thought senselessly to herself. You can never see the rainbows in the woods. Just the rain.

He showed her the locations of a dozen salt licks, where the trampled grasses testified to the patronage of salt-hungry deer.

'I thought salt licks were illegal,' she said, bending to finger the well-defined prints of a particularly large deer.

'Only when you use them to lure animals in for the kill, and that doesn't happen here. Every inch of this land is posted now. It's a refuge, not a trap.'

'Oh my!' she whispered in alarm, standing quickly, backing away from the lick with widened eyes. 'It's a bear, isn't it?' she asked tremulously.

He stepped forward to examine the deep circular indentations in the soft ground. 'Definitely,' he nodded. 'Black bear, probably, and a male, I'd guess, from the size of the print.'

'Oh my,' she repeated foolishly, feeling the blood drain from her face. She was unconsciously sidling over towards Haveron, and jumped and spun when she bumped into him. 'Sorry,' she said breathlessly, staring at him; then she started to shake her head. 'How stupid,' she whispered, her eyes glazed with the full reincarnation of a childhood fear. 'How incredibly stupid! I never even thought about the bears. In all the years I dreamed of coming back, all the excitement about spending a year alone in the woods, all the dreams—God! I forgot about the bears!'

She became a child then, a quivering, frightened child, and Haveron's arms went round her instinctively. She trembled in his embrace as she had in her father's years before, when he'd comfort her after a nightmare; then a strong, responsive chord reminded her that years of independence separated her from that child, and that the weak never survive anywhere, especially in the forest.

'I'm sorry,' she said, pushing away from him abruptly. 'It's not like me to give in to fear like that. Especially not such a childish one.'

She kept her eyes averted until he placed large hands gently on either side of her face, turning her head to look at him. The green of his eyes was soft with concern and sympathy and tenderness, and for the first time in her life Jessie didn't resent the protective impulse she saw in a man's face.

'It has to be a black bear,' he said softly, and his voice seemed to travel through his hands to enter her body, setting the pathways of her nerves thrumming like the string on a bass guitar. 'We have one that I know of which winters on the land, but that's all. There used to be a lot more, but even then they rarely showed themselves to humans.' His voice dropped to a whisper. 'They're not nearly as aggressive as the grizzly, for instance, or even the brown bear. You could probably meet one on a path and walk away unharmed.'

'No, I couldn't,' she whispered back, mesmerised by the eyes that somehow seemed to be swimming closer to hers, lost in a blurry, faded background. 'I'd die of fright on the spot.' The eyes *were* getting closer. She could barely see the rest of his face now, only the eyes, flashing forest-green with a growing circle of bottomless black, opening wider and wider until she thought it could encompass her whole body, if she just leaned forward and fell into it. 'He wouldn't have to lay a paw on me,' she whispered senselessly, watching the extraordinary phenomenon of his eyes, her lips parted in wonder.

And then there was a soft touch on her lower lip—not a pressure, exactly, more like the passing brush of a butterfly wing, so quick and light she wasn't sure she'd felt it at all; and then there was another, and another, and the string of the bass guitar swelled to a full symphony, blossoming with heat and sound that exploded in her stomach and shot up to her breasts and throat and escaped from her lips in a tiny, inaudible exclamation just before his mouth closed on hers. She felt the band of his arms tighten convulsively as his lips opened against hers, and then an instant later the heat and the pressure vanished as he jerked his head up and backwards, and her eyes fluttered open to focus on the visible beat of the pulse beneath his jaw.

CHAPTER SEVEN

JESSIE huddled in front of the lodge fireplace, her knees drawn up to her chin, her thoughts dancing as erratically as the roaring blaze that warmed her.

'Stay by the fire,' Haveron had ordered when he left for the kitchen to make something hot to drink; and for the first time since her childhood she was happy to do precisely as she was told. Besides being thoroughly chilled by the long walk through the damp woods, she felt a desperate need to be alone long enough to make sense of her thoughts—something she could not seem to manage in Haveron's presence. It wasn't only the man that made her uneasy; it was her reaction to him.

She had responded to Haveron's embrace with an urgency that alarmed her, following the instincts of her body without a single conscious thought of what she was doing. That fine edge of control she had spent most of her life mastering had vanished instantly under the touch of his hand, and the realisation that she could be so easily led horrified her. Perhaps it was all tied in with returning to this place, she reasoned calmly. Perhaps it wasn't really Haveron at all, but simply a combination of all the emotional stimuli dredging up memories from her past. It wasn't so strange, really, that she should reach out for the comfort of another human being when those dark memories awakened. And it probably didn't matter who that person was. It could have been anyone. Haveron just happened to be there.

She pulled in a deep breath and tightened her arms round her legs, reaching down into her subconscious for the detachment that had ruled her life for the last twenty years. You're fine, she told herself sternly. You're just fine, just the same as you've always been.

Just because you were moved by a man doesn't mean you're losing control.

But she'd been shaken by that spontaneous union with a man she barely knew, and she'd been grateful when he'd tramped silently on through the woods as if it had never happened. Ignoring what had passed between them seemed to render it harmless—one of those brief, inexplicable episodes that are better left forgotten, like a summer romance, or the jolt of meeting a stranger's eyes across a crowded room. But as they moved through the pathless underbrush, stopping every now and then to examine a favoured watering spot, the silence between them became heavy and awkward. It drew attention to the fact that the last time they had spoken they had been in each other's arms; and eventually it seemed as if time had stopped when they had touched, and that, no matter how far they walked, they would never be able to leave that one moment behind.

Jessie felt an almost ludicrous urge to call her mother, to make contact with that world she had left behind, hoping it might reconnect her with the Jessie Loren she felt slipping away—that cool, detached, intensely private Jessie who bore very little resemblance to the person she had been today. But what would she say? Listen, Mother; I met this man, and he threatened to shoot me; then I nearly ran over him on my bike; then I told him all my secrets and he kissed me and we haven't exchanged a word since. Now what do you think of that?

She tossed her head angrily, then closed her eyes in frustration. She'd been out of control since she'd first seen the lodge again, responding to stimuli like some dumb animal, unable to predict her own actions. She had never intended to share with anyone the agonising memories of her mother's breakdown. That was a part of her past that no one else had ever seen, or was ever meant to see. Yet she had paraded it before Haveron as if he had pushed the magic button, forcing her to reveal the deepest parts of herself. What was it about this man she barely knew that could demand such painful honesty?

'Warming up?'

He'd done it again; appeared magically next to her without a single sound to warn of his coming. She willed herself not to jump and looked up at the tall, dark figure at her side.

He bent from the waist to hand her a steaming mug of cocoa, his expression as stiff as his movement was fluid. 'Here. This should help.'

She nodded her thanks, accepting the mug and cupping her hands round its warmth.

He lowered himself gracefully to a cross-legged position, then moved back from the fire almost immediately. 'Lord, that's hot. How can you sit so close?'

She inched even closer to the hearth, lengthening the distance between them. 'I don't think I'll ever be warm again. My heart may belong to Michigan, but my body belongs to California. It'll take some time to adjust, I think.'

'My fault,' he said into his mug. 'We were out much too long, and you weren't really dressed for it.'

She dismissed the apology with a slight shrug, intent on the fire before her, disturbed by the simple fact that he was sitting within arm's reach.

After a long moment of silence, he made a quiet observation. 'You are without a doubt the most uncommunicative woman I've ever met. Do you realise you've barely spoken all afternoon?'

Neither have you, she countered to herself before answering. 'I think I more than made up for that with my ramblings before lunch. Believe it or not, you know more about me than any person on earth, after just one day.'

'I believe it,' he said softly, then fell silent again.

She sipped cautiously at the rich, frothy chocolate, turning slightly to eye him over the rim of her mug. He sat facing the fire, his eyes riveted to the flames that cast a kaleidoscope of darting shadows across his features. His lips were compressed into a hard line that accentuated the sharp angle of his cheekbones; and even without the slightest shift of expression his face seemed to make a strong, almost violent statement about the man behind it.

She had been about to say something; but now, looking at him, the words flew from her mind like a flock of startled sparrows taking wing. She stared at him unabashed, deep brown eyes wide and intent, her lips parted slightly over the rim of her mug.

No wonder you can barely control your thoughts in his presence, she thought with something akin to relief. It isn't just your reaction to him as a man; it isn't anything as frightening as that.

Suddenly she could identify her responses to him, and in this new light of revelation they seemed harmless. It was like encountering an artistic masterpiece in the flesh; trying to make idle conversation with a subject one never expected to be real.

You don't even think of him as a man, she told herself, relaxing now that she had her feelings all neatly categorised. He's just one of those once-in-a-lifetime artistic subjects, waiting for your brush.

'Am I being appraised?'

She could not have been more startled if the Mona Lisa had spoken. 'I'm sorry,' she stammered, carefully setting down the mug she had almost spilled. 'It was rude of me to stare like that.'

He shifted his eyes to look at her without moving any other part of his body. 'You do it often,' he said.

She dropped her gaze immediately and fidgeted with a loose thread at the seam of her jeans, feeling a flush of embarrassment. 'It's just professional interest,' she said quickly, trying to regain her composure, reaching for that sense of relief she'd felt just a moment before. She took a deep breath and forced her eyes to meet his levelly. 'I'd like to paint you, that's all. I wouldn't want you to think . . . it was anything else.'

He laughed out loud, but it was a mirthless, unpleasant sound. 'Good Lord! Why would I?'

Jessie frowned, wondering why he would say such a thing. A man who looked as he did must be used to women clustering about, drawn to that rare aura of pure masculinity he exuded constantly. In fact, she thought, if I had to describe him in one single word, it would be masculine, and nothing attracts women more. No, she amended, assessing him openly now; masculine isn't the right word. That implies humanity, and he's more animal than human. The right word is 'male'.

'You're doing it again.'

She blinked slowly, surprised by the sound of his voice, and by the astonishing turn her thoughts had taken. Something is happening here, she thought nervously. Something very strange is happening here.

He still hadn't moved. He was still sitting cross-legged, his arms draped casually across his knees; only now he was staring at her, and the thought struck her that the green of his eyes was very unnatural, almost inhuman.

'You're uncomfortable here, aren't you?' he asked.

'Yes,' she breathed. 'I guess I am.'

'Why? This is your home, after all.'

'No,' she said sharply, shaking her head so strongly that her hair swung around her shoulders in a half-circle. 'It's your home, now. And you're the man who shoots trespassers, remember?'

'I never kiss and shoot,' he said. 'It's unsporting.'

She smiled at that, relieved that he could make reference to what had happened between them so casually. It reinforced her feeling that it had been meaningless.

'Besides, I don't think fear of being shot is what makes you uncomfortable. Not now, anyway.'

He watched her carefully for a long time before he spoke again. 'At any rate, you needn't worry about being shot. Not by me, at least. The grounds are yours.' He lifted his shoulders in an elegant shrug. 'You belong here as much as I do.'

She caught her breath and stared at him. Oh, thank you for that, she said inside her mind. Thank you for putting it quite that way.

She could not have known that the gratitude she felt at that moment was written clearly on her face; that it was the sight of that feeling softening her eyes, touching her lips, which made him straighten slightly and jerk back.

'Why the sudden change of attitude?' she asked carefully. 'Yesterday I was a common trespasser; today you're serving me cocoa and giving me the run of the place. Now how do you account for that?'

He relaxed visibly, and she thought she caught a slight curve at the corners of his mouth, as if he were concealing a dark smile. 'What if I told you my intentions were less than honourable?' he asked quietly. 'What if I told you I had simply decided that I liked the idea of being stranded up here all winter with a beautiful woman?'

She made a little face at the preposterous adjective, but decided to ignore it. 'I wouldn't believe you.'

'Why not?'

'Because you don't seem like the type of man who would swayed by anything so. . .'

'Human?'

My God, he knows everything I'm thinking, she thought. Then she shrugged. 'Maybe. So what's the real reason?'

One side of his mouth lifted in amusement; then without warning he turned in a half-circle and leaned back until he was stretched full-length beside her, his head resting just inches from her legs. 'The real reason was your art,' he murmured, locking his hands behind his head, extending long legs to cross at the ankle.

'Oh,' she said dully, unaccountably nervous to have him suddenly stretched out before her. He looked so . . . exposed, so vulnerable, lying there like that; and yet somehow dangerous, with every line of the tight body advertising its potential to spring into immediate action.

'We have a lot in common,' he continued, shifting his hips to a more comfortable position, watching her eyes as they jerked quickly to the source of the movement, then even more quickly away. 'I could see just how much in your sketches this morning. It was all you needed to say.'

With a suddenness that made her jump, his hand shot out to grasp the back of her neck. His eyes searched hers briefly, then there was a firm, unrelenting pressure, pulling her down until her face was poised above his, close enough to feel the heat of his whisper. 'Perhaps you over-estimated me, Jessie Loren. I may be more human than you think.'

Her body remembered the last time they had been this close, even if her mind had tried to forget. She exhaled sharply at the sensation, as if all the breath had been drawn from her lungs at once. There was no rational reminder that this man was a virtual stranger; no thought of independence, strength, or pride. There was only the tempo of her body responding to the closeness of his. There was no room for anything else.

She hung motionless over him, waiting for the strength which she knew was in that hand to pull her downward those last few inches; aching for it to happen, knowing full well that she could end this here and now by simply pulling away, but not choosing to do that. Then, as suddenly as his hand had taken possession of her neck, he lifted it away, freeing her from any pretence of coercion, forcing her to decide.

Bewilderment touched her brow in the instant her face remained suspended over his, then disappointment, then fear. As long as he had been touching her, she had no freedom of choice. She was blessedly relieved of that obligation by a body that simply responded, helpless to do otherwise. But this was different. He was demanding her initiative, her choice, a conscious commitment to actions that would demand relating to another human being—the one thing Jessie had feared most in all her life. Closeness to a man would end with pain, and dependence, and weakness. Her own mother had shown her that with a lesson she was not likely to forget.

She straightened quickly, watching him as carefully as she would have any other potential danger.

'You're afraid,' he said with unexpected gentleness, one brow lifted in mild surprise. 'I didn't think you were afraid of anything.'

'Except bears,' she reminded him in a frantic attempt to shift the subject of their discussion.

'Does that mean I'm in the same category as my giant black friends?'

She looked nervously at the mocking green eyes, thinking that at this moment he did indeed seem giant, dark, and dangerous. 'No, of course not,' she lied. 'I just don't understand what's happening. I don't understand your feelings, or your motives, or anything about you.'

He pulled himself up to a sitting position, turning to face the fire. 'That's not quite true, Jessie. I think you know a great deal about me, and that's what scares you.'

She looked at him sideways in genuine bewilderment. 'What are you talking about? How could I know anything about you? I can barely remember you as a child, and all I've seen of the adult Haveron is a cold, uncaring. . .' She hesitated then. Yesterday that had all been true; but today? Was the man who kissed her really so uncaring? The man who had told her she belonged here as much as he did?

His profile softened almost inperceptibly as she watched, and for the first time his voice was hesitant when he spoke. 'Precisely. Cold, uncaring . . . just like you. You've just described yourself, you know. We're like mirror images of one another. I felt that the first time I saw you.'

Her eyes widened as she remembered that first, troubled recognition when she met him. 'I'm not uncaring,' she whispered, and he turned and looked at her intently.

'I know that. And neither am I. It just looks that way.'

She closed her eyes in a pained acknowledgment of all the times when she, too, had been accused of being cold; of all the times when she had wished that just one person in the world knew that the hard exterior was necessary to protect the fragile remnants which hid inside. But now that it had happened, now that a stranger had seen through the veneer to the uncertain woman beneath, she found that she wasn't ready.

'I have to go,' she said nervously, jumping to her feet, half-expecting that he would try to stop her. When he merely sat there, looking up with a quiet, knowing gaze, she felt foolish.

'Look,' he said gently, rising to his feet to face her, 'it's been a long day for you. How about a belated welcome to the neighbourhood, such as it is? A steak? A little wine?'

She looked up at him warily, hearing the distant clang of an alarm bell deep in her mind, but her lips would not form the words of a polite refusal. She wanted to stay too much.

'There's nothing to be afraid of here,' he said, answering her unvoiced fears. But he looked very tall, and very dark, and very powerful standing next to her tiny frame, and she questioned the truth of those words. Then he smiled a slow, beautiful smile that cleared his brow and made him appear boyish and innocent, and Jessie's heart responded with a fluttering thump.

'Wait until you see me in an apron,' he said kindly. 'I won't seem nearly so intimidating then.'

CHAPTER EIGHT

As it turned out, he wasn't entirely right. He mastered the kitchen with the same cool, masculine precision which he exhibited anywhere else. The apron he donned temporarily did little to conceal the controlled energy of his movements, or the dark undercurrent of violence that seemed to emanate from him constantly.

Jessie perched on one of the kitchen stools, watching him frown at the steaks on the grill. He paused to brush a shock of dark hair from his eyes with one forearm, and the angry impatience of that gesture made her shiver. There was a barely suppressed rage in the man. It was evident in every movement, every glance, no matter how controlled; and she wondered what he would be capable of if the violence ever broke free.

She twirled the stem of her untouched wineglass idly, not nearly as fascinated with the crystalline pink liquid as she was with the man at the grill.

'You haven't even tasted the wine,' he said without turning.

'I'm not much of a drinker, actually.'

His chuckle was low and just a little bit condescending. 'It's only a light rosé, and it might help you to relax a bit. You're much too tense, you know.'

There was no reason to bristle at his observation. It was nothing less than the truth, after all. She didn't resent being so easily read nearly as much as she resented being tense at all. It was an unfamiliar, thoroughly unpleasant sensation. Maybe he was right. Maybe a little wine wouldn't hurt.

She sipped delicately at the liquid and found it surprisingly good, although there was a peculiar tightening at the back of her neck after only one swallow.

'Like it?' He still hadn't turned away from the grill, but it didn't surprise her any more that he seemed to know precisely what she was doing without even looking at her.

'As a matter of fact, I do. But I think it makes me more tense, not less. I can feel it in my neck.'

'That's only an initial reaction; a measure of how tight your muscles really are. It'll go away in a minute.'

Jessie was no stranger to the effects of alcohol. She'd seen enough companions give way to foolishness after over-indulging, and had always been very nearly paranoid about reaching such a state herself. The thought of losing control had been a looming spectre that had limited her consumption to a cautious sip at most. But tonight she felt the tension more than she felt the fear of losing control, and allowed herself to enjoy the wine. By the time she'd finished half a glass, Haveron looked a good deal less formidable, and she felt more at ease than she had all day.

She smiled a little and looked up to find his eyes on her. 'We seem to spend a lot of time staring at each other, don't we?' she asked honestly.

'Actually, I was thinking that you must have looked a lot like you look now, sitting in this very room as a child, watching your mother cook.' He closed his eyes briefly, as if the thought of her as a child had been somehow painful. 'Well. If you'll find a suitable table in the dining-room, I'll bring the food.'

There was something very binding about breaking bread together, Jessie thought later. No matter how uncertain you were about someone, eating was a common denominator that brought everyone rapidly to the same level. Seeing that Haveron required sustenance just like any other living creature made him seem much less frightening. Even though they had passed the meal in relative silence, she was beginning to feel more comfortable with him, almost friendly.

Still, when he suggested that they finish the bottle of wine by the fire, she was happier to select a single chair safely above his own seat on the floor.

'Do you feel safer up there?' he asked, reading her thoughts, mocking her with a half-smile.

'Actually I wasn't thinking of safety at all. I think I'm finally beginning to relax.'

He leaned back against the couch opposite her, locking his hands comfortably behind his head. 'Probably the wine.'

She lifted her shoulders in a careless shrug that dropped a long sweep of her hair across one breast. His eyes lingered on the fan of brown shimmering in the firelight, but his gaze was so impersonal that she remained unconcerned.

'Did you know that your hair is exactly the same shade of brown as your eyes?' he asked. 'Exactly.'

Suddenly the fire seemed much too warm.

'More?' He lifted the wine bottle and his brows in inquiry.

She hesitated, then held out her glass. 'Why not? I don't suppose two glasses of wine will make me any more of a fool than I've been already today.'

His brows nearly touched as he filled her glass. 'You think you were foolish today?'

'By my standards, yes.'

'Because of what you remembered about the bears . . . and your mother?'

'Because I had an audience for memories that were . . . very personal,' she said flatly.

He stared at her intently for a moment, then drained his own glass and refilled it. 'I'm sorry you feel that way,' he said simply, and a shadow passed across his face, as if he had been disappointed somehow. It disappeared before she could be certain she had seen it. 'Tell me,' he continued lightly, 'what started you drawing? School?'

'Oh my, no. Loneliness.'

Once the word was out, she couldn't call it back. What had made her say that? She'd never even articulated the thought to herself. 'I was never much of a socialiser,' she went on hurriedly, trying to cover her embarrassment even as her babbling made it worse. 'And I was never happy in California. Drawing was my escape, I think. Back to when my father was alive, and my mother was happy. Back here. Home. I just painted myself home.'

She turned away from his gaze quickly to stare into the flames, pressing the fingers of one hand to her forehead. The words had just fallen out. She'd had no control over them whatsoever. He'd asked her a simple, casual question, and she'd responded by baring her soul.

She felt naked, defenceless, helpless to employ the closed answers she always used with everyone else, the answers that revealed nothing.

'Sorry,' he said, noting her distress. 'I didn't mean to pry.'

She looked up at him in confusion. He hadn't pried. Not really. He'd just raised his hand to tap lightly at the door. She'd been the one to fling it wide, exposing everything inside.

'Were you always lonely?' he asked quietly.

There was a flicker of warmth—or was it pity?—in his eyes that she didn't like.

'Were you?' she shot back, wanting to hurt, wanting to drag confusion from him, wanting to see the pain of his past as he had seen hers.

'Of course,' he answered simply, and because he didn't even try to conceal the pain, the need to see it vanished.

'Oh, God,' she moaned. 'I don't know what's wrong with me. I'm telling you things I barely know about myself. Talking without thinking, without. . .'

'Deceit?' he finished for her. 'Is that what's bothering you? That you're confiding in me, a stranger, when you've always found it impossible to confide in anyone else?'

She hesitated, frowning, then nodded her head reluctantly. 'Yes. That's exactly what I'm doing, isn't it? Confiding in you as if I'd known you all my life, and I don't know why. I've never done that with anyone. Ever.'

His eyes were two bright pinpoints of green, fastening on hers with an intensity that rocked her. 'Then I thank you for that,' he said with quiet sincerity. 'Being trusted is an extraordinary experience for me. I only wish it weren't so disturbing for you.'

His face lifted in a smile that made him look totally benevolent, totally worthy of anyone's trust. 'You're tense again,' he pointed out, nodding to where her hands clutched at her knees.

She bent her head forward and turned her hands palms up, looking at them as if they had betrayed her. Her hair fell forward in a curtain on either side of her face, making her feel closed in and protected. But then the hair was pushed back, and he was kneeling in front of her, his face mere inches from hers, searching her eyes with that penetrating gaze which seemed to look down to the very deepest part of her mind. But this time there was a return, she realised, staring at his face in wonder. This time she could see him too; and with a start she understood that this was because he was allowing it. He had put the barriers aside, discarded the mask that hid the man, and for the first time she was looking into the face of the real Haveron Michels, the man her instincts had known was there all along.

Her hands went to his cheeks of their own volition, and she let herself fall into the depths of the strange green eyes. His lids closed at her touch and his forehead creased in an expression that could have marked either pain or defeat, or a little of both. This was the face of the man she had confided in; not the remote, rigid mask that had confused her, but this kind, compassionate face, with the silent strength born of sorrow and wounds that would never quite heal.

'Haveron,' she whispered, wanting the eyes to open, wanting to see if they too would reflect the man she was seeing.

The lids lifted slowly, and let her inside. 'You see, Jessie?' he whispered. 'I know you, and you know me. We've known each other all our lives. We've travelled the same road, felt the same pain and the same isolation, and nobody knew.' He stared at her in quiet wonder. 'I can see myself in you. I can look at your face, and know that I don't have to tell you anything, because you know it all already. I've waited all my life to see that in another person's eyes. I just never thought it would happen.'

She felt the restrained strength of his arms as he grasped her shoulders and guided her to the floor, cradling the back of her head as he lowered it, then caressing her face with the hesitant wonder one feels with the newborn.

'You feel it,' he murmured, searching her eyes almost desperately for the confirmation of his hopes. 'My God, you feel it, too. It's real, isn't it?'

She knew she was seeing a part of this closed, suspicious man that no one had ever seen before; that as surely as she had inexplicably revealed herself to him, he was now doing exactly the same to her. Instinctively they had opened their vulnerability to each other, offering themselves like sacrificial lambs on the altar of a trust that neither had experienced before.

She could only lie there, helpless to resist the rush of long-buried emotions that pulled them both along an unfamiliar course. Her lips parted in a moist circle as she watched the dark face descend to hers, his eyes narrowed in almost painful contemplation. Tendrils of his hair brushed her forehead and she felt a responsive shudder travel through her body, even as their eyes remained locked together in a mutual wariness that would linger until the last moment. Then his lips grazed hers and her eyes fell closed in welcome resignation, and the sensations of her entire body rushed to the tiny circle that was her mouth, moving it against his, finding the focus of her being in the small part of her that was now joined to him.

He drew back to look at her, his arms quivering as they braced against the floor on either side of her, his nostrils flaring slightly with the silent force of his breath. His eyes travelled the course of her face with the astonished reverence of a man who has found water after an endless period of thirst; and Jessie responded to that look with a rush of warmth which began below her stomach and rushed up to fill her breasts. Her own feelings were so violently intense that when he lifted one hand to caress her face she was surprised at the gentleness of his touch. His fingers trailed from her brow to touch tentatively at the corner of her mouth, and then down to span the slender column of her neck, emphasising with the large circle of his hand the contrast between male strength and female resistance.

He could snap my neck with one hand, she thought seneselessly; and just a short time ago I felt he had the violence in him to do just that. But now his touch was delicate, coaxing, and she tipped her head back as his hand moved down to the swell of her breast, catching her breath with a tiny gasp as he pressed against it, following his hand with the arch of her body as it slid down to her stomach, lifting into it, straining towards it.

'You belong to me,' he murmured thickly, staring into her eyes, sliding his hand beneath the bulk of her sweater and up to where the mounds of heated flesh were rising and falling in an ever-increasing tempo. She stifled a cry as his fingers brushed over the aching peak of sensitive tissue, not denying his words of possession, not even resenting the ownership they implied. Women did not belong to men, nor men to women. That's what independence was all about. No one could own another human being. She knew that. She had lived that, all her life. But now, at this moment, with his hands slipping down to her jeans-clad thighs; with his chest suddenly flattening her breasts beneath it; with his leg sliding insistently between hers; she belonged to Haveron, and he to her, and nothing could have seemed more right.

He breathed her name in a hoarse cry just as their

lips met, and she lifted her hips to his in a rocking explosion of desire. Then suddenly he jerked his upper body away, locking his elbows to support his weight. His eyes were still and watchful, lifted towards the fire, his breath caught and held in his throat.

Fear stabbed through her, the same fear that strikes any female animal when her mate senses danger. She blinked rapidly, searching the face that hung over hers, vaguely aware that their lower bodies were still pressed together, throbbing in unison. 'What?' she whispered, wincing when he silenced her with an abrupt shake of his head.

In a motion so swift and silent she could barely register it, he was off her, standing rigidly erect, his head lifted with the tension of concentrated listening. Even with the fire crackling behind her, she felt a strange coldness settle where his body had been. She wanted to ask what he had heard, but did not dare break the tension of his silence for fear of masking any other sound. So she lay there immobile, feeling strangely naked even though she was fully clothed, straining to hear whatever it was that had pulled him so cruelly from her.

His head jerked suddenly to the side and his lids half-closed over eyes gone dark and still with alert patience. Although his chest still lifted with the ragged reminders of his desire, his breathing was perfectly silent. And then she heard it too; the uneven clatter of something tumbling just outside the front door, falling against the side of the porch.

Her heart leaped with an immediate, ridiculous thought of bears, and she sprang to her feet with the swift silence her body remembered from her youth.

He lifted one hand, palm out, to keep her still, his eyes brushing over her rapidly. He must have seen the fear in her face, for he took time to cup her chin in the gentle reassurance of his hand before moving silently away through the large room, past the registration desk, and over to the front door.

The hairs on the back of Jessie's neck prickled with apprehension, and she moved quickly to follow him, ignoring the disapproval in his dark gaze. When she was at his side, facing the closed door, he placed one hand on the porch light switch and the other on the doorknob. He turned it slowly, his eyes narrowed to slits of concentration, then jerked open the door and flicked the switch in the same instant.

Jessie's hand flew to her mouth to cover her cry, and pressed hard until the flesh around her fingers whitened.

There, just a few yards from the porch, several logs from the woodpile lay scattered at its base, as if something had tried to clear the towering stack with a leap that fell short. Crumpled on the wispy grass among the scattered logs was a young doe, frozen by the light that had blinded her, the buff beauty of her luxurious coat marred by the ragged streaks of blood running down her shoulder. Jessie could just make out the feathery tips of the arrow that pierced the tender flesh high on the shoulder, dangerously close to the spine; but before she had time to completely take in the grisly tableau, the doe began a frantic struggle to rise.

Her hind legs were scored with scratches that testified to her panic-stricken flight through the underbrush, yet she managed to bunch them beneath her haunches to support her weight, and in one frantic thrust she regained her feet. She turned her head towards the porch as she fought for breath, that pained, liquid gaze seeming to invite the end if it would be forthcoming; then her front legs buckled and she fell hard on her knees with an agonised grunt.

Jessie grabbed Haveron's arm convulsively, barely registering the angry, bunched muscles beneath her fingers; and in that moment the doe made one last gallant effort, struggled again to her feet, and staggered off into the woods. Her passage was marked with that sickly, crashing sound made only by a wounded creature heedless of all obstacles.

There was blood on the grass where the deer had fallen, and Jessie couldn't take her eyes off it. She just stood there with her mouth still open in a silent cry, unshed tears glistening in her eyes, her hand still locked round Haveron's arm. Haveron. She'd almost forgotten him.

She turned to look up at his face, fully expecting it to be as twisted with horrified compassion as her own, and jerked back when she saw the stranger standing next to her. She felt a distant prickling at the base of her spine which she recognised as fear, because this was not the gentle face of the man who had caressed her so reverently just a few moments ago. Nor was it even the face of rage that had chilled her so that first morning they'd met. It was a different face altogether, a different man; and he terrified her.

'Haveron?' she whispered, carefully loosening her grip on his arm, hoping that the sound of her voice would bring back that other man, the man she had wanted to love.

His face remained expressionless, in that not a muscle moved across its length and breadth. His eyes remained fixed on the circle of blood on the grass.

'Haveron!' she said more urgently, shaking a little at his arm so that he would look down at her. But when he did, when he turned his head slowly on his neck and dropped his eyes to meet hers, she wished he hadn't.

The eyes were still, lightened now to a pale, icy green that seemed very nearly colourless, as if his humanity had been contained in that deep, rich green, and both had been drained from him. His lids were half-closed, like a partially drawn blind that conceals the worst from an unsuspecting world. There was a force in those eyes, a determined violence which screamed from the depths of the chilling calm that looked at her now without seeing, and Jessie was afraid.

'Haveron?' she whispered uncertainly, shivering as the cool night air finally touched her senses, chilled even more by the look in his eyes.

'Yes.' The word rumbled from unknown depths. It acknowledged her presence, and at the same time seemed to dismiss her existence as unimportant.

'What can we do?'

He seemed to focus on her then, for only an instant, then his eyes grew distant again. 'We can do nothing. I can do a great deal.'

Then he spun out of the circle of her vision and disappeared into the side room that had once been the office of Jessie's father. Light spilled into the foyer from the room when he flicked the switch, and Jessie paused long enough to push the front door closed before following him timidly.

Even as nostalgia pulled at her heart to see that room exactly as it had been twenty years before, the more immediate dangers of Haveron's actions dragged a sick fear through her stomach.

'What are you doing?' she asked, taking one step into the small room, blocking the doorway.

'What has to be done,' he said tonelessly, shrugging into the heavy jacket which he pulled from a wall hook.

Her heart sank when he crossed to the massive gun rack and lifted a short-barrelled rifle from its brace.

Look at me, she implored silently, wanting to make contact with the man behind the mechanised figure now pulling the bolt, inspecting the chamber, and sliding the deadly missiles inside. Please look at me.

It was clear that he had already decided the deer would have to be shot, and even though she knew he was probably right, she felt she had to make at least a token protest. She needed to hear that there was no other way; that the beautiful animal was beyond help; that killing would be a kindness.

'Does it have to be done?' she asked in an unnaturally small voice.

The dark hair hanging over his forehead bounced and quivered as he rammed the bolt home. Then he looked up at her, slowly, a look of mild surprise in his face as if he'd forgotten her presence entirely.

He straightened to his full height, broadened by the heavy jacket, and Jessie felt the power contained in his form—almost thought she could see it, surrounding him like an aura of blackness.

'She didn't travel far with that wound,' he said, his voice flat, machine-like. 'That means she was hit on my land. Out of season. *On my land.*'

'Haveron. . .' She held out her hand and he jerked backwards away from it, startling her. 'Haveron, maybe we could save her. Maybe you could save her. You used to do it all the time, you used to. . .'

'Jessie.' The word was soft, patronising, and his chilling smile never touched his eyes. 'If you're going to worry about anything, worry about the hunter, not the doe,' he said quietly, and Jessie's mind reeled with the impact of his words. He had no intention of tracking the deer. He was going after the hunter.

'Haveron, no!' she breathed, reaching out to snatch at the rifle, never considering that she was no match for his strength. He jerked the gun easily beyond her reach, then swept out his other arm as he passed her, slamming her body painfully against the doorframe. She doubled over, clutching at her mid-section in a fruitless effort to hold in the air that had already escaped, but he never noticed. As she looked up through the curtain of hair thart had fallen over her eyes, she caught a glimpse of his rigid profile as he passed. He hardly knew she was there.

'Haveron!' she gasped. 'You can't do this! You can't hunt down a man, no matter what he's done; you just can't! It's murder!'

He stopped and turned his head slowly to glare at her, his face still expressionless. He smiled coldly at her stricken silence, and then he was gone.

Jessie slid to the floor in a daze, horrified by the vision of violence perpetuating violence, twisting those it touched into the haunted, ugly forms of vengeance. It had happened to Haveron, right before her eyes, and she had been helpless to stop it.

She sat huddled against the doorframe, deep brown eyes glazed, her hair lying in tangled disarray around her shoulders. He was wrong, she thought sadly. We're not at all alike. I have nothing in common with the man who just left here, pushing me aside as if I didn't exist.

But the man by the fire, her mind persisted—he touched you, and you touched him. But perhaps he wasn't real, she countered her own thoughts. Perhaps he had never existed, that gentle man by the fire. That may have been the mask, the disguise, hiding the real Haveron, the man she had just seen.

She pushed herself tiredly to her feet and listened, for a moment, to the silence around her. She felt very small, very insignificant, in the enormous, empty lodge; and her broken sigh echoed in a dozen rooms where there was no one left to hear.

CHAPTER NINE

JESSIE did not leave the lodge—she fled from it, running headlong through the night towards her cabin, pitching forward to her knees more than once when she stumbled. Racing beside her was the vague reminder that there were at least two armed men about in the dark woods tonight, and that her hurrying, indistinct figure might be mistaken as a target by either one of them. Her father's accidental death had demonstrated all too clearly the price of mistakes in the woods.

She stopped dead on the path halfway between the lodge and her cabin, her chest heaving, cursing herself for the mindless rush that had sent her out into the darkness without a flashlight. At least a light would have advertised that she was not a deer, saving her from the poacher; and since poachers didn't want their presence known, the light would have saved her from Haveron, too.

My God, I don't believe it, she thought dully. After everything else that's happened today, now you have to worry about being struck down in the middle of the night by an arrow or a bullet, mistaken for either a wounded deer or a poacher.

She closed her eyes in despair and tried to control her breathing, alert for any sounds around her that didn't belong. But you wouldn't hear Haveron, she reminded herself with a shiver. He *does* belong. He's as much a part of the woods as any of its creatures, and in his present state of mind, easily the most dangerous. No matter how much he might regret a shot fired at her by mistake, it would still leave her just as dead.

She forced her trembling legs to move forward, pursing her lips to try for a whistle. When that failed, she began to hum tunelessly, the sound ragged with the nervous breaks of her breath.

Moonlight broke fitfully through the towering pines, scattering shadows across the path in front of her. The forest was unnaturally silent, as if holding its breath, waiting for the black and white drama to unfold.

Jessie jumped when a twig snapped off to her right. She caught the next note of her humming painfully in her throat and froze into a tiny statue dwarfed by the trees. 'Don't shoot!' she cried, and the words echoed foolishly in the quiet that followed.

Just an animal, she told herself nervously, her eyes wide, trying to peer through the blackness. Probably a rabbit, or a racoon, or even a bird moving on its perch, or a bear. . .

She had never thought of bears until that moment, and suddenly the very air around her seemed alive with sinister presence.

'There, you see?' she said aloud, her voice shaking with a fear that threatened to overcome her. 'You don't have to worry about two armed madmen shooting at anything that moves. They'll never get you. They won't have a chance. You'll be torn apart by a bear first.'

She felt an insane giggle building, threatening to rise from her throat and fill the silence with its crazy melody; and somehow that frightened her most of all. She commanded muscles frozen with fright and sprinted the last few yards to the cabin, flinging open the door, slamming it safely shut behind her, then crumpling where she stood to gasp weakly on the floor.

After a few moments she stiffened, seeing herself as she must appear, frightened, shaking . . . weak. A wave of revulsion passed through her body, eradicating the fear, replacing it with anger. She shot to her feet, flicked on the lights, and strode purposefully back to the bathroom.

'Oh God,' she moaned, disgusted by the pathetic creature the mirror reflected. That once smooth sheet of her hair, as solid and controlled as its owner, had flown into mad tangles which streaked across her face and stood out from her head. Her face was a sickly shade of white, blotched with two high points of colour on cheekbones so sharply etched it looked like they had been drawn there. And her eyes, detached and coolly placid only this morning, were huge, dark orbs in the white of her face, looking entirely too large for the tiny pinched features.

'Cute,' she muttered angrily at the mirror, pushing back the tangle of her hair. 'Tough, self-sufficient Jessie Loren, falling apart after a couple of days in the wilderness. Frightened by your own shadow. You could handle the city, the muggers, the hustlers, late hours, poverty, and a mother who went mad while you watched; but you can't handle a short walk through the woods.'

She was being too hard on herself. She knew that, but the sound of her own voice was a comfort. She berated herself through a long, hot shower, pulling all her fears, real and imagined, out into the open where she could deal with them. By the time she finally crawled under the covers an hour later, she felt more like herself. She could sense the sharp edge of control slipping comfortably back into place, and when the fear was finally gone all that was left was the grief, and the disappointment in her own poor judgment. She had seen something magical in a man who was truly as cruel and uncaring as her first impression had warned her. But she'd wanted him to be more; wanted it so desperately that she'd closed her mind to the obvious.

'You're a cold, unfeeling bastard, Haveron,' she murmured into her pillow. 'Especially for pretending you weren't.'

It was difficult to fall asleep. Part of her consciousness struggled to remain alert, half-listening for the sound of a rifle shot to shatter the night. She would jump if she heard it, she knew; and she would be sickened by what the shot would mean. Whether Haveron found the doe or the man, a shot would mean that a living creature was dead.

Did it matter, she wondered crazily as she drifted off?

Did it matter which creature died? Wasn't life equally precious to both of them? The thought that that might have been what Haveron felt shot through her mind so quickly that it was gone before she could examine it. Besides, it was beneath consideration. That was what made Haveron crazy, thinking an animal's life was worth a man's. She welcomed unconsciousness as it drew closer, hoping it would erase from her mind the heart-rending picture of the wounded doe.

Jessie shot straight up in bed, every sense alert, the tiny hairs all over her body quivering with warning. She felt the strain of her eyelids pulling as wide as possible, trying to pierce the darkness of her room. Then she was fully awake, and let her lids fall closed so that she could devote her total concentration to sound. Her eyes squeezed shut with the effort of trying to hear, but there was no sound at all save the heavy thudding of her own heart. And that was wrong. The forest was filled with night sounds; at least it should be—unless something had silenced all the creatures with fear.

She opened her eyes slowly and shifted them to the luminous dial on her bedside clock. 3:30. Too early for that natural pre-dawn hush which sometimes quiets nature while the sun hangs suspended on the horizon. There should still be night sounds.

Jessie eased out of bed and padded to the window, wincing when the floorboards creaked under her weight. When the sound finally came, it startled her so badly that she gripped the sill convulsively, and felt the wood slide under palms clammy with sweat. But then the sound came again; too loud, too obvious to be the stealthy movements of any stalking predator. Somehow it sounded more desperate.

She frowned and reached for her heavy terry robe, pulling it over the clinging stickiness of her nightshirt. Now the sound was almost continuous, punctuated by the periodic grunts of a large animal struggling for breath. She grabbed a flashlight from the night table and directed its beam out of the window, jumping back in alarm when it reflected two red orbs less than ten yards from the cabin wall.

'Oh, no,' she cried, grabbing the flashlight with both hands to steady it.

The doe lay just at that point where the wall of woods met the cabin's clearing, one hind foot caught in a tangle of roots that would have been no obstacle at all for a healthy animal. But this creature's strength was gone. She lay on her side, ribs heaving with the effort of painful breaths, blood still oozing from the angry wound that marked the arrow's entry into her shoulder. She lifted her elegant head weakly, and seemed to stare at Jessie where she stood peering out of the window, the large eyes reflecting red in the flashlight's beam. Then the eyes glazed over and the head fell heavily to the ground.

'No,' Jessie whispered, dashing away the moisture that had sprung to her eyes, scrambling for moccasins she had left by the bed. 'No, no, no.'

Then she was rushing silently through the dark cabin, easing outside, as noiseless in her desperation as she had been naturally as a child, her mind remembering the ways of the woods she thought she had forgotten.

She crept silently up to where the doe lay, playing the flashlight's beam over the tortured body, speaking softly to warn of her coming. 'It's all right, lady, beautiful lady, I won't hurt you, please don't run, don't try to run. . .'

She knelt cautiously by the magnificent head, and at that moment the delirious doe focused on the warning of her instinct, and made a last valiant effort to flee. She scrambled with hind legs that were too weak to support her, grunting with the enormous cost of her pathetic effort. Finally she stilled, just a flicker of awareness still alive in the polished eyes, resigned at last to a fate she was no longer able to protest.

Jessie had leaped up and back, away from the frantic thrashing; but now she crept forward again, speaking soothing nonsense, reaching out with one hand. 'There, there, beautiful lady, be still, be still, I only want to help, shhh, shhh. . .'

She felt the tremble of weakened muscles as her fingers brushed the thick hair of the doe's neck; then there was a convulsive shudder under her palm as she stroked gently with her whole hand. 'You see? It's all right. You don't have to be afraid any more. I won't hurt you. I promise.'

She huddled there in the chill night, feeling the warmth of life ebbing away beneath her hand, tears streaming unnoticed down her cheeks. 'Hold on, lady,' she murmured, still stroking the neck. 'Hold on. I'll help you. I'll get help, and you'll be fine, and no one will ever hurt you again, I promise. But you have to trust me, you just have to, or you don't have a chance. Please, please don't die.'

She straightened slowly, still talking softly, easing away from the doe with only one thought in her mind: that of a sullen, angry boy tending the wounded creatures of the forest; healing them, erasing all but the scars of their tortured encounters with man.

'I'll be back,' she said senselessly, for the doe had sunk into the blissful painlessness of delirium. Then Jessie turned and began to run.

She banged on the front door of the lodge until her fist was an angry red, clutching at the pain in her side, gasping for air between screams. 'Haveron! Haveron!'

Finally the door jerked open under her fist and she tumbled forward into his arms.

He grabbed her shoulders and pushed her back far enough to look down at her face. 'What the hell is this?' he bellowed; then he saw the flood of tears that wouldn't stop, the pained expression that cried out silently to him, and his brow creased with concern. 'What is it? Jess? What is it?'

She took a deep breath and swallowed. 'Hurry! You have to come . . . the deer . . . at the cabin. . . .'

He shook her lightly, pressing his fingers sharply into

the flesh of her shoulders. 'Is she still alive?'

Jessie nodded weakly, then staggered as he raced away, calling over his shoulder for her to wait. She sagged against the doorframe, her shoulders heaving with the force of her gasps for breath, but he was back before she could slow her heart, a heavy leather bag slung over his shoulder.

'Go!' he barked, supporting her elbow, rushing her down the porch stairs and back to the path.

'Can you run?' he asked brusquely, shining a flashlight on to the path before them.

She closed her eyes briefly, ignoring the shooting pain in one leg that warned of a cramp, then sprinted away with Haveron close at her side. Within minutes they approached the cabin's dark bulk, and he grabbed her elbow and jerked her to a halt. The sudden stop nearly sent Jessie tumbling to the ground, but he steadied her with a firm hand on her arm, waiting while she regained control over her shaking limbs. She nodded once to indicate her ability to go on, then led him to within a few yards of where the doe lay. Her sides still heaved in the light.

'She's alive,' Haveron whispered incredulously, shining the light on the angry wound. He closed the last few yards slowly, speaking the same nonsense as Jessie had in a similar, soothing tone; but the doe shot to life at the sound of his voice, thrashing at the forest floor with her legs.

'No! No!' Jessie cried softly, dashing forward to kneel at the deer's head, restraining the weak thrusts of the muscled neck with the simple touch of her hand. 'No, no,' she whispered again, as the tears that had dried in the run once more flowed freely. 'You mustn't move, lady, you musn't. Please, please be still so that we can help.' Jessie bent until her hair swept the ground, her eyes mere inches from the exhausted, wary gaze of the doe. Then her cheek touched the hot, dry muzzle and the doe blinked once, very slowly, and stilled with a shuddering sigh.

Haveron stood quietly immobile, watching the incredible drama, his eyes touching first the deer, then the huddled, weeping form beside her. His lips compressed slightly, and his eyes were strangely bright.

'Come on, Haveron,' Jessie sobbed without turning to look at him. 'Come and work your magic, damn you.'

'All right, Jess,' he said quietly, and she felt the deer tense momentarily under her hand. 'But keep talking to me. Let her hear both our voices.'

'All right. It's all right. Come closer.'

His voice interspersed with hers until the deer associated them both with the same presence, and then Haveron could approach her. When he finally knelt at her side, she jerked only once at his touch, then permitted the steady hypnotic stroking of his hand on her neck. Perhaps she had grown used to the sound of his voice; or perhaps she was past caring, for she lay there unmoving, her mouth slightly open as she pulled for air.

'She's dying, isn't she?' Jessie whispered sadly.

'She's very close.'

'Can you do anything?'

'I don't know. She's lost a lot of blood. But I'm sure as hell going to try.'

He produced a syringe from the mysterious bag and rubbed more firmly on the doe's neck, then injected the contents close to the distracting motions of his hand.

'What was that?'

'A sedative. We have to get that arrow out.'

'Are you a vet?' Jessie asked, stunned by the sudden realisation of how very little she knew about this man.

He just shook his head impatiently, and bent to his work.

Dawn crept so softly into the woods that Jessie was unaware of its arrival until Haveron told her to turn off the flashlight.

'Almost finished,' he said, dusting the last of the

superficial scratches on the doe's hind legs with antibiotic powder. 'And I think she might make it. This lady is a fighter.'

Jessie heard an uncharacteristic tremor in his voice, and looked over at him. The dark stubble of a beard washed the lower part of his face with the same colour that circled his eyes. There were white lines of exhaustion pulling at his mouth and creasing the corners of his eyes, disguising any other emotion he might have felt. 'Can you help me move her?' he asked, glancing at her doubtfully.

'Of course I can,' Jessie said without thinking; then smiled to hear those old familiar words jump forth so readily. 'Where to?'

'Just over there, where the sun is hitting the ferns. The dew has collected around her here, and she needs to be warm and dry.'

'Can't we take her inside?' Jessie begged. 'Or at least confine her somehow? She'll run away when she wakes up, or try to.'

Haveron rose stiffly and shook his head. 'She'd die in any kind of confinement. She'd be terrified, and the fear would kill her now. She's too weak.'

'But. . .'

'Besides, I'll keep her sedated for the next twenty-four hours. It'll give her body the time it needs to rest.' He bent to slide his hands under the doe's front quarters, then looked up through the fringe of hair that hung over his eyes. 'Don't worry, Jessie. She won't run, or even try to. I promise.'

Between them they managed to ease the dead weight over to the sunny fern bed without disturbing the newly-stitched wound. After she had satisfied herself that the doe was breathing deeply and normally, Jessie struggled to her feet, pressing her hands to the ache in the small of her back.

'You did well,' Haveron said quietly, nodding at her.

Jessie looked down at the neatly-stitched wound where the arrow had been and shook her head. She remembered gasping when she had first seen it closely.

The doe's panicked flight had apparently jostled the arrow's shaft time and again against tree trunks and branches, moving the blades inside her body, enlarging and tearing the original wound. 'It made me sick,' she said slowly. 'I never knew arrows did that.'

Haveron's lips tightened into a grim line. 'They always do that,' he said quietly.

The whole episode had taken on the quality of a nightmare in the bright light of a new day, and if the doe hadn't been lying there before her, Jessie would have wondered if it had ever happened at all.

'Where did you learn so much about medicine?' she asked.

'From an old vet in Alaska. I lived with him for a few years.'

'Alaska?'

He dismissed her questioning with a brief smile. 'I'll tell you about it some time, but right now I could use some coffee, and your kitchen's closer.'

She led the way jerkily towards the cabin's front porch, her aching legs threatening to give way with every step. She stopped dead at the point where the doe had fallen and stared down at the discarded arrow, its lethal tip black with dried blood. She bent from the waist to pick it up, slowly, like a sleepwalker, then held the instrument of death in one hand while she gazed at it. 'Did you find him?' she asked Haveron.

'No.'

She remembered the deer's innocent agony, her fear, her own flight to the lodge and the long hours that had followed. 'God forgive me,' she said woodenly. 'I almost wish you had.'

They started the coffee maker, then moved to the living-room to wait until it finished brewing. Jessie sank into the recliner and Haveron flung himself on his back on the old patterned couch. Jessie saw him move once, when he threw his forearm over his eyes; then she felt her own eyelids drooping, and thought that coffee makers were never fast enough when you really needed them.

CHAPTER TEN

JESSIE wakened naturally this time, her eyes fluttering open to focus on Haveron as he watched her from the couch.

'What time is it?' she asked sleepily.

'Ten o'clock. A little after.'

She jerked forward in the chair as the memories rushed in all at once. 'The doe. . .'

'Relax. I just checked on her. She's still sleeping.'

It wasn't that she didn't believe him. She just had to see for herself. She shrugged an apology and tiptoed outside.

'It seems so unnatural,' she said when she came back in a few moments later. 'I've never seen a deer sleep before. The only time I've seen one that still was when it was. . .'

'Dead. I know. But that's exactly what she needs now, natural or not. The only thing better than sleep would be a transfusion, and I'm afraid I don't have that kind of magic.' He smiled a little to be using her own words, and she smiled back.

'I always thought of you that way when I was little, you know,' she told him. 'Like a mysterious, miniature medicine man working magic spells to cure the animals.'

He shook his head and smiled. 'I was just a kid.'

'No. You were never that.'

He stared at her thoughtfully for a moment, then shrugged the subject aside. 'I made a new pot of coffee while you were sleeping. Come on. We'll drink it dry.'

It was only when they were sitting across from each other at the tiny kitchen table that she realised what a picture they made. She was still in her nightshirt, the now filthy terry robe just barely preserving decency, and she could only guess at what her face looked like. Haveron's was dark with new beard, still showing strain round the eyes. He wore a pair of jeans and nothing else under the jacket he'd snatched on their way out of the lodge so many hours before. It hung open now, exposing a broad chest that tapered down to a tightly muscled stomach.

He caught the direction of her gaze and looked bemused. 'We weren't exactly dressed for a night outside, were we?'

She shook her head and sipped at her coffee, staring at him openly. He lifted his brows in a silent question.

'I'm just trying to decide which man you are,' she cautiously.

'What are your choices?'

She hesitated for a moment, biting down on her lower lip. 'The gentle, sensitive man who worked all night in the cold to save the life of a dumb animal, or . . .' she paused and dropped her eyes, '. . . or the hard, frightening man who walked into the night with a gun, prepared to use it.'

His stare was hard and unflinching. 'In other words, the good guy, or the bad guy.'

She nodded once.

'Well, the two certainly don't mesh,' he said tonelessly. 'It would seem that one of your assessments is wrong. Now all you have to do is decide which one.'

It wasn't the response she had expected, or hoped for. She'd wanted him to protest the darker picture; to proclaim himself the gentle man; to explain away his behaviour last night with a reason she could understand. Instead, he was forcing a choice on her—again.

He looked away with an expression she interpreted as disgust, then rose quickly from the table. 'I need some things from the lodge, and I'd like to clean up. I'll be back within the hour. Have you had a chance to lay in any supplies yet? We're going to need some food.'

She nodded silently.

'Good. I'll spend the day here, and tonight, at least.

That should take the doe through the critical period. If it makes you uncomfortable to have me here, you can stay at the lodge.'

'I'd rather stay here and help, if that's all right.'

His mouth twitched in a grim smile. 'Of course it's all right. The cabin is yours, after all. And if last night was any indication, so is that doe.'

Jessie was outside with the deer by the time Haveron returned, and she only realised his presence when his low chuckle made her jump and look up.

'I can see that you showered,' he said softly, walking over to lift a strand of her wet hair, 'and that it was pointless.'

She followed his gaze to her hands and the knees of her clean jeans, already soiled from kneeling. She looked up with a child's chagrined expression. 'I can't stay away from her,' she explained sheepishly. 'She's so beautiful, and so . . .' she looked down at where her hand rested on the firmly muscled neck, '. . . helpless.'

'I'm reducing the sedative,' he said with sudden, inappropriate brusqueness. Jessie watched, wincing as he pierced the neck with the point of a hypodermic. 'I want her relaxed, but conscious enough to drink, at least. That's the next milestone. She's going to have to take in fluids soon, or we'll lose her to dehydration.'

His hand cupped her elbow as he helped her to her feet. 'Come on inside. It's time we both had something to eat. She won't budge for another hour or so.'

Jessie resisted the pull on her arm. 'Are you sure she'll be all right?'

He tipped his head to one side and looked down into her eyes, his own narrowed with concern. 'I'm sure about the doe. I'm not so sure about you.'

He touched the delicate, darkened tissue under her eye gently with one finger. 'You look exhausted.'

He's beautiful, Jessie thought later, watching him eat across the kitchen table. There simply isn't another word for it.

The dark stubble was gone from his cheeks and chin,

and there was one small nick on his jawline marking the razor's passage. His hair fell in thick, full sheets over his forehead and ears, still damp from the shower, darker than ever. The strange green eyes were quiet now, like the depths of a silent forest pond, bearing no trace of last night's rage.

'You forgot about bears,' he said, breaking the sounds of their meal.

'What?'

'Bears. You ran all the way to the lodge in the middle of the night without worrying about bears.' His mouth quirked in a teasing smile that faded immediately with her next words.

'I was more worried about other beasts roaming the forest last night,' she said flatly. 'A bear seemed pretty harmless compared to two armed men.'

He stirred the soup in his bowl absently, but two white lines appeared at the corners of his mouth. 'I didn't mean to frighten you,' he said, staring at the mindless circling of his spoon.

'But you did.'

He pinched the bridge of his nose between thumb and forefinger and sighed heavily. 'Let's forget about that, shall we? There's nothing now that will change what happened last night.' Then he looked up at her pointedly. 'Any of it.'

Her heart skipped a beat as his words recalled those incredible moments by the fire when he had been tender and she had been giving, both of them totally out of character.

'You're not getting much painting done, are you?' He changed the subject awkwardly.

'No. I suppose not. But they won't be expecting anything this soon. I have time.'

'They?'

'The magazine that's paying for my year here. They've commissioned twelve wildlife paintings for their annual calendar. The advance money will buy the groceries until I get the first piece shipped, then they'll send more.'

'I hope you're getting what you're worth.'

That pulled a smile from her. 'And what would that be?'

'I'll tell you someday,' he said simply.

They nursed the deer together throughout the first day, and Jessie felt her uncertainties about Haveron slipping away every time she saw him with the doe. His touch was unbelievably gentle, and the extent of his compassion was etched clearly on a face strained with concern. More than once Jessie stopped an impulse to reach for his head, to cradle it against her breast in an almost maternal gesture. She could see the boy in the man who knelt over the buff-coloured body; his hair tousled, his brow furrowed, his entire being focused on working that little-boy magic of healing; and the boy touched her deeply. Was this that quivering tower of rage she had met the night before? Had those gentle, sensitive hands cradled a gun and carried death through the forest? She could not merge those two contradictory personalities, and so, as he told her she must, she made a silent choice. And then she fell in love.

By late afternoon the doe eased up from unconsciousness and turned a trusting gaze upon Jessie as she supported the elegant head over a bowl of water. They had to refill the bowl three times, and when Jessie looked at Haveron, and saw his smiling nod of approval, she lowered the head gently down to the pillow of ferns. She stroked the short hairs on the doe's brow until the huge eyes closed once more, then she turned a magnificent smile up to the man who watched her so intently. He turned from her quickly and went back into the cabin.

'You draw, I'll cook supper,' he told her curtly when she followed him in.

'I don't feel like drawing, but you can still cook,' she said happily, all dark thoughts banished by the doe's improvement.

He poured canned chilli into a pot on the stove and began slicing a loaf of bread.

'That's not cooking,' she chided him, sliding into a kitchen chair.

'Someday I'll treat you to my homemade chilli, when there's more time.'

'Someday, someday; that's all you ever say. Someday you'll make chilli, someday you'll tell me about Alaska . . . you're racking up a lot of somedays, Haveron.'

'So I am,' he said, 'but the winters are long here. We'll have time.'

It was such a promising thing to say, conjuring up all sorts of images of long, fireside evenings and intimate conversations. Suddenly Jessie felt a surge of unfamiliar foolhardiness, as if she were about to open a door she would never be able to close again.

She looked at the back he had turned towards her as he worked at the small stove, her eyes following the clean line from shoulder to waist to long, straight legs, set slightly apart now; and she felt an embarrassingly sharp reminder of what that body had felt like pressed against hers. She wanted him to touch her. Just sitting there, looking at him, she felt her breasts swell against the rough fabric of her shirt.

He turned without warning to look at her, and she blushed as if he had read her thoughts.

'Can I at least set the table?' she asked too quickly.

'No. I'll do it.'

'You'll spoil me.'

'It's time somebody did, isn't it?'

It was an oblique, unintentional reference to that male instinct which Jessie had hated all her life; that deep, primeval need all men possess to protect and care for their women. But suddenly, in some small ways, the idea of being a woman who needed a man wasn't all that hateful. Certainly now, with those unnatural green eyes piercing the very heart of her, she felt more feminine—no, more *female*—than she ever had in her life.

My God, she thought as her lips parted. I want him. In that most basic, elemental way; I want him. Cold and cruel, or tender and gentle—it didn't matter any more which was the real Haveron. Not now. Not at this moment. Right now all she cared about was the feeling that engulfed her whenever she looked at him. No pride, she screamed silently to herself. No pride at all. What's happened to you?

But it didn't matter. At least it wouldn't, if only he would touch her.

He set bowls and plates on the table, his hands moving within inches of where she sat, his body leaning towards her as he reached across the narrow expanse of wood, and then away when he straightened.

He has to know what I'm feeling, she thought when he paused to look at her, trapping her with a look of amused speculation. It must be written on my forehead, the feeling is so strong.

But if he did, he gave no indication of it. He just smiled faintly and turned away, tugging at her heart with every movement of his body as he served the meal.

After a silent supper she went into the bathroom and recoiled from the image in the mirror. 'Oh brother,' she moaned sadly, staring at her reflection. No wonder he'd found it easy to remain so detached. There was very little to attract in her pale, tired face, her untidy hair, the boyish clothes. Before she realised what she was doing she had piled her hair on top of her head and was applying the first make-up she'd worn all day. Then she went into the bedroom and shed her jeans and shirt in favour of a long lounging robe that plunged dangerously at the bodice, exposing the creamy rise of both breasts.

Suddenly the image in the dresser mirror disgusted her, and, unobtrusive as the make-up was, she felt like a whore, painting her body to sell to the highest bidder. She went back into the bathroom and scrubbed at her face until it was shiny and pink, pulled the clips that released her hair from its preposterous perch on top of her head, then strode angrily into the living-room. She was no Delilah; no temptress of any kind. Her life had never permitted the luxury of developing such skills;

and until tonight she had had only contempt for the women who practised them. Now she felt contempt for herself for succumbing to those very same instincts, for her pathetic desire to reinterest a man whose ardour had obviously cooled. The hell with him, she thought angrily. Until she looked at him.

He was crouched in front of the fireplace, prodding a reluctant blaze with the poker, brushing impatiently at the dark hair falling over his forehead. The poker jerked to a sudden halt when he turned to look at her, and hung suspended and useless over the flames. His eyes swept down from her face to that point where flesh met bodice and lingered there. Jessie blushed furiously, knowing that he couldn't miss the sudden rise of her breasts, cursing herself for forgetting to discard the robe along with the make-up.

'It's comfortable,' she shrugged angrily, not realising that the shrug lifted her breasts even further from the loose garment, exposing more of them to his quiet gaze.

'I'm sure it is.'

He turned his attention back to the fire, and suddenly it all seemed so silly. Jessie sighed, releasing the tension of thwarted passion, and walked to the front door.

'I'm going out to check on her.'

'You've checked her every half-hour all day,' he said quietly.

'I know.'

'Well, grab a coat then. It's cooling off already.'

Her thoughts shifted totally to the doe. 'Should I cover her?'

He chuckled and shook his head. 'No, she'll be fine. She's sheltered from the wind in that hollow, and she has a fine coat already.'

Jessie shrugged into a jacket and padded out to the doe. She stirred slightly under Jessie's touch, opening one eye sleepily before drifting off again. 'So beautiful,' she whispered, stroking the thick hair on the neck. 'So beautiful. I'm falling in love again; twice in the same day.'

She closed her eyes in despair when she heard the words spoken aloud, thinking how right she had always been to avoid involvement of any kind. It was just as painful as she had always suspected it would be, and not just with people, either. She would pay dearly for her unwilling attachment to this doe. She knew that already. If she recovered completely, one day she would bound out of Jessie's life, leaving her to wonder and worry for as long as the memories survived, and memories survived a very long time. Even those first, childish loves left a pain that was never completely erased. Jessie had received her first scar when she was only five years old.

Her mother had brought home one of Hazel Meerchamp's puppies as a companion for Jessie: a plump bundle of tan she had promptly named Ice Cream after her favourite dessert. She smiled and shook her head, remembering. Coffee ice cream. She'd been addicted to it then, and the pup had been exactly the same colour, just like this doe. She had doted on that puppy, pouring every ounce of her childish love into that buff fur ball, and when he had disappeared one day her devastation had been total. She didn't eat or sleep for days, and when her mother tried to replace the pup with another Jessie would have none of it. Even then, at age five, she had known that she couldn't stand the pain of such a loss more than once.

'And now I'm doing it again,' she whispered to the sleeping doe, pressing her cheek against the fine muzzle. 'And I swore I never would.'

'Hey.'

She jerked her head up to see Haveron standing next to her. 'Dammit! I wish you'd stop sneaking up on me all the time!'

'Sorry,' he frowned. 'But you've been out here a long time. I'm not sure who needs watching more, you or the doe. And look at you. Down in the dirt again. You're going to ruin that dress.'

He was treating her like a child, and she hadn't been one of those since she was eight.

She strode into the cabin ahead of him and went straight to the tall kitchen cupboard next to the stove. 'I'm going to have a drink,' she snapped, pulling out the bottle of vodka Walt had packed for her in spite of her protests that she would never use it. She grabbed an orance juice bottle from the refrigerator and slammed it down on the counter next to the vodka; and then she stopped, chewing her lip in angry frustration.

'What's the problem?' Haveron was leaning against the kitchen doorframe, his arms crossed over his chest. 'I thought you were going to make a drink.'

She spun on him, eyes flashing, feeling every bit the child his treatment implied she was. 'How much of this stuff do you put in?' she demanded, and although she wouldn't have blamed for laughing, he didn't.

'I'll do it,' he said seriously. 'Maybe we both could use a drink.' There was a glitter of amusement in his eyes as he glanced at her over his shoulder.

'Better?' he asked her later in front of the fire; and although it was better, and the drink was helping her to relax, Jessie hated to admit it. It was just one more sign of the weaknesses she'd been piling up in the last two days.

She slouched on the sofa, staring disconsolately into the remaining liquid in her glass. 'I think I have real potential as an alchoholic,' she said miserably.

'After two glasses of wine and one drink over a twenty-eight-year period?' He chuckled and shook his head. 'I'm afraid you don't qualify.'

Her gaze sharpened and she looked up at him. 'How did you know how old I was?'

'Shrewd calculation,' he tapped the side of his head with one finger. 'You left twenty years ago, the same year I left, and you were eight then.'

She sighed and looked over at the fire. 'Why did you leave here?'

'It was time,' he said quickly, his eyes darkening.

'But you were only—what? Fourteen? Fifteen?'

'That was old enough.'

'You hadn't even finished school yet.'

'I did that later.' He paused, shaking his head at some memory that still troubled him; then shrugged, discarding it. 'My mother occupied herself with other things after the lodge closed. I was definitely in the way.'

Jessie frowned a question, and he smiled coldly. 'She had a very simple philosophy, my mother. You either had a job, or you had a man. That was basic survival. The man she found after she lost her job was a hunter, and I didn't quite fit in with the two of them.'

'So you just left?'

'Actually they left first. Detroit, I think. At least, that's what the note she left said. I heard later that she'd been killed in a car accident of some sort, but by the time it was like hearing a stranger had died. We were never what you'd call a close, loving family.' He laughed harshly at his own understatement, and Jessie shivered at the bitter sound. Even if she had lost the security of caring parents at an early age, at least she had had it once.

'Then what did you do?'

'Oh, I worked the ore boats for a few years; took a few correspondence courses; spent some time in Alaska; and then I came back here.'

Jessie smiled doubtfully. 'That isn't much of a description for twenty years of time, and it doesn't explain what you do now, or where you came up with the cash to buy this place. I get the feeling you've left a few things out.'

'Maybe a few,' he said coolly, effectively shutting her out.

Suddenly she felt like the intruder again, someone who had yet to prove they were worthy of trust. Apparently that fleeting sense of oneness she had felt last night was entirely one-sided—or perhaps he had something to hide.

'Well,' she said lightly, 'will Ice Cream need another shot tonight?'

'Ice Cream?' he asked, his brows lifted in amused disbelief. 'You named her Ice Cream?'

'What's wrong with that?'

'Well—nothing. It's just such a . . . well, it's not a name I would have expected you to choose, that's all. It's so. . .'

'Juvenile. I know. But she's the same colour as a puppy I had once, when I was very very young. I named him after coffee ice cream, and we have to call her something.'

He smiled a little and shook his head. 'Coffee ice cream. It sounds disgusting.'

'It is just this side of Heaven,' she protested righteously. 'At least, I used to think so, and that is the very last deep, dark secret you will ever learn about me.' Her lower lip protruded in a pout that was not entirely affected, and he laughed out loud, filling the cabin with the vibrant sound of his voice lifted in pleasure.

Jessie felt the familiar tingle along her spine and fought it for as long as she could, then she said seriously, 'I've never heard you laugh before. Not like that. I didn't think you could.'

'You're obviously a very inspiring lady,' he said, his mouth quirked into a little smile. 'And if there is a better side of me, I think you bring it out.'

She smiled crookedly and shrugged. 'What are friends for?'

And then suddenly he stilled, and the air in the cabin seemed oppressive and thick.

'We can be that, at least, can't we?' Jessie asked in a small voice, thoroughly puzzled by his rapid change of mood. 'Friends?'

He stiffened, staring at her with an odd expression; then he nodded. 'I guess we can,' he said rigidly.

'Well. That will take some getting used to,' she said with forced lightness. 'I've never had a friend before.'

'That makes two of us.'

CHAPTER ELEVEN

JESSIE woke at dawn the next morning, disorientated because her bedroom clock was not in its proper place. Then she remembered that Haveron had taken it to the couch in the living-room to waken for the periodic checks on the doe.

She felt a tremor of excitement just to think he was in the same house, but she quelled the feeling as quickly as it had arisen. They were friends, as far as he was concerned; and even that he had agreed to with a reluctance which hurt her more than she wanted to admit.

She pulled herself from bed with a curious mixture of disillusionment and anticipation, as if the day didn't promise to be much, but still held a chance for improvement.

There was a heaviness in the morning air that foretold one of those last, precious warm days before the autumn chill arrived in earnest. Jessie dressed for it in lightweight jeans and a peasant blouse that draped loosely over her shoulders in a gentle scoop. She pulled her hair back into a long ponytail that accentuated the smallness of her features, making her face seem delicate and childishly feminine in spite of her sober expression.

'Haveron?' she called to the empty cabin, and when she received no response she went immediately outside.

'Oh. There you are.'

He looked up from Ice Cream's side, his hair endearingly tousled, his smile rueful. 'And where else would I be? It would seem that my entire life is consumed with dancing attendance on two ladies. For the last couple of days, anyway.'

His words were only a gentle tease, but Jessie frowned uncertainly, not certain how to react.

'Oh, stop looking so sombre,' he chided her. 'Here. Take a look at our patient. I'm beginning to think you were right about me. I'm a magic healer.'

He stood away from the doe, and amazed delight flooded Jessie's face as she looked down at her. 'Oh, she's awake!' she murmured, moving quickly to crouch at the doe's head, fighting the impulse to throw both arms around the lovely neck. Instead she stroked the lifted head gently, thrilled that this wild creature not only tolerated her touch, but seemed to welcome it.

The doe lay more on her stomach now, legs tucked beneath her in a more natural pose, and the large, soulful eyes were quietly alert. She regarded Jessie calmly, her slow, languid blinks communicating a trust born of necessity, and growing with the passage of time.

'She's going to make it, isn't she?' Jessie asked.

'She's not out of the woods yet,' Haveron answered carefully. 'She still has a fever, and in spite of all the disinfectant we poured into the wound, there's bound to be infection. She'll be weak for a long time yet.'

'What can we do?'

'The antibiotic shots are about the best we can offer. We'll keep her on those for as long as she'll tolerate them. But in the meantime she needs to take in some nourishment, and plenty of water. We'll have to wait on her until she can get around enough to forage for herself.'

Jessie rose without a word and began to walk straight for the forest.

'Hey. Where are you going?'

'To get food for her,' she called over her shoulder.

Haveron hooked his thumbs in his front pockets and shook his head with a little smile. 'And what does a deer eat, Jessie?'

She hadn't even considered that. Deer eat grass, don't they? And leaves, and things like that? But what kind of grass, and what kind of leaves?

'All right!' she said in irritation, stopping and turning to face him. 'So you tell me. What do I look for?'

He hefted the large leather bag to his shoulder. 'I have alfalfa pellets at the lodge, and some cracked corn, and a little bran. We'll start her on a mash of that before we move on to roughage. I need more antibiotics anyway, and some food for us. We've just about depleted your limited stores already.'

She looked down at where her foot scuffed back and forth in the dried grass, feeling unaccountably foolish. 'I'll do some more shopping today. I suppose it's time to stock up anyway.'

Haveron looked up at the sky speculatively. 'You're right about that. We won't have many of these days left.' He started walking down the trail towards the lodge, then stopped suddenly and turned to look at her. 'By the way,' he said, 'I like your blouse.'

Jessie stood there uncertainly long after he had disappeared from sight, wondering why she was blushing.

Haveron had only been gone a few minutes when she heard the unnatural rumble of an engine rolling up through the woods from the direction of the road. Her first concern was that the noise would frighten the doe, but Ice Cream apparently felt secure enough to reflect only mild interest by twitching her comically large ears; or perhaps she was still too weak to panic. Jessie left her to walk round to the front of the cabin, shading her eyes to look down the trail at the pick-up lumbering towards her. Her face lit up as she recognised the truck and the bright blond head of its driver.

'Toby!'

He climbed down from the cab with an uncertain smile, obviously puzzled by the welcoming look on Jessie's face. He had pegged her as a loner; a distant, reserved woman who would take a very long time indeed to form attachments. Her obvious pleasure to see him again was a distinct surprise.

'Well,' he drawled, ambling towards her with his large hands shoved deep into the pockets of his denim jacket. 'The only explanation for that dazzling smile is that you're desperate for the sight of another human being. I haven't had time to work my charm on you yet.'

Jessie grinned at the amiable, open face, a little puzzled herself that she should be so pleased to see this blond giant again. In a way, the past two days had taken on the murky quality of a nightmare; as if she had been trapped in an isolated world where everything seemed slightly unreal, especially her own feelings. But Toby, with his healthy good looks and his endearing, uncomplicated smile, seemed a sudden, welcome contact with the outside, a return to normalcy. She felt more sure of herself in his presence than she had in days.

'It's good to see you again,' she said simply. 'Can I offer you something? Coffee?'

'You read my mind. I ran out this morning and haven't had my quota yet. And that's really why I stopped. Mr Ellis told me you were toting groceries home on your bike. Since I had some shopping to do anyway, I thought I'd offer to take you in the truck. It'll hold a lot more than what Mr Ellis calls your useless little red wagon.'

She laughed easily as she led the way back to the kitchen. 'You're a life-saver, Toby. That's just what I need to do today.'

It was so easy to sit at the kitchen table, sipping coffee with this man, chatting like any two normal people getting to know one another. Toby was almost half again the size of Haveron, with a husky, football player physique that dwarfed the tiny kitchen; yet his presence was not nearly so tangible or so troubling as that of the slimmer, more intense man. Jessie was totally comfortable, and almost giddy with the relief of being with someone so open and uncomplicated. There were no dark mysteries about Toby; no quicksilver mood changes or dangerous undercurrents. She almost sparkled in the ease of his company.

'So,' he said after they had exhausted the small talk

about weather and what she would need at the store, 'I hear you made contact with the man himself.'

'Haveron, you mean?' She remembered talking about their first meeting at Mr Ellis's store, but somehow that seemed like something that had happened a very long time ago. 'Yes, you might say that. He's a strange man, Toby. Just when I think I'm beginning to understand him, he changes into someone else.'

Toby leaned forward on his elbows and frowned. 'You mean you've run into him more than once?'

Jessie rolled her eyes and laughed, then told Toby an abbreviated version of the two days that had seemed like a lifetime. She left out anything that might have revealed the turmoil of her feelings—especially that first night by the lodge fire—but she described the incident with Ice Cream in detail, ending by taking Toby to her bedroom where he peered out of the window at the sleeping doe.

'Well, I'll de damned,' he murmured, shaking his head in disbelief to see a deer so close to the cabin. 'I didn't know a man like Haveron could ever take the trouble to care about anything.'

His voice registered disbelief at her account of Haveron's solicitous care of the doe, and Jessie knew that it didn't mesh with all the dark tales Toby had heard about him. She felt a fierce loyalty that was totally unfamiliar, and elaborated on Haveron's gentleness, as if it were her responsibility to shift Toby's opinion.

He watched her carefully as she spoke, his blue eyes sceptical, then piercing, and then strangely resigned.

'Well,' he said when she had finished, 'I'll tell you the truth, Jessie. I took one look at you at the station that morning and laid out a whole plan of attack in my mind.' He grinned and shook his head at her. 'I thought I'd ease into your life real slow, since you seemed a little suspicious, but eventually I planned to make myself irresistible. I can see now that I waited much too long to make the first move.' He laughed with the good nature of a man who accepts defeat gracefully. 'Who'd have thought that, with a lady like you, one lousy day could make so much difference?'

'I don't understand,' she said warily. 'What are you saying?'

'Oh, Jessie.' He reached out to cup her chin in the curve of a huge palm. 'You're bewitched by the man. You'd have to be a blind fool not to see that.'

She stopped the indignant denial before it reached her lips, and her shoulders sagged a little. 'So much for secrets,' she said miserably. 'So much for that invincible exterior I've been cultivating for all these years.'

He shook his head with a sad little smile. 'I'm not the town crier, Jess. Your secrets are your own, if you can keep that moon-eyed expression off your face when you talk about him.' He walked to the front door and turned to her with a sigh. 'I'll say one thing. He must be a hell of a lot more than any of us thought to win you over so fast. Now come on. Let's get your shopping done.'

Mr Ellis was delighted to see her again so soon, and helped Toby select a veritable mountain of supplies that they both insisted she would need to get through the coming winter. She shook her head at the laden boxes as Toby carried them into the cabin when they returned.

'You let Mr Ellis think we were seeing each other,' she chided him gently when the supplies were finally all stored away.

'No need to fan the gossip fires too soon,' he answered with a shrug. 'At least that'll keep the townsfolk off the scent for a while. You've got to remember, Jessie; Haveron isn't a popular figure around here. They hold him personally responsible for the drop in hunter traffic the last few years, and being linked with him isn't going to make you any friends. And you might need friends, come winter. It isn't easy up here, you know, once the snows lock out the rest of the world.'

'But I've got one friend, haven't I, Toby?' she asked.

'You do,' he smiled through his dark blond beard. 'But I could have been a lot more than that. Lady, you don't know what you missed.'

They laughed together as they walked back outside.

'Hey,' he stopped suddenly on the porch. 'I almost forgot. You didn't show me any of the calendar paintings you were talking about.'

'I haven't done any yet. There hasn't really been time. But you'll be the first to see them once I get started.'

Toby raised one blond brow and she laughed. 'All right. Maybe the second.'

'I guess I'll have to settle for that. I only hope Haveron knows what he's got. By the way, you'll have to let me know where I can get one of those calendars when they're finally printed.'

'That's easy enough. Just subscribe to *The Wild Life* magazine. My agent tells me the calendar comes free with the subscription.'

Toby's brows came together, clouding the affable face. 'Yeah, I know. I get that magazine. Most everybody around here does. So that's the calendar you're doing.' He turned slowly towards the truck, then back to face her, his expression uncertain. 'Tell me, does Haveron know what you're doing up here?'

'You mean the calendar paintings? Sure. I told him that. Why?'

Toby shook his head in obvious confusion. 'Oh, I don't know. I just wouldn't expect him to like the idea, that's all.' Then his face cleared and he shrugged. 'But you'd be the woman to turn him round, I guess. Okay if I stop by every now and then? Just a friendly visit or two, to see how you're doing?'

'Any time, Toby. And often. I love having you around,' she smiled.

'You may regret that invitation. I might just decide to throw my hat into the ring anyway, Haveron or no Haveron.'

She gave him an amused glance that said precisely

how futile such a gesture would be, and he laughed out loud. 'In the meantime,' he confided, 'I may have to console myself with a particular bright-eyed lady who works at the diner every now and then. Something tells me my prospects are considerably better with her.'

Jessie laughed and stepped easily into the outstretched arm that snugged her close as they walked to the truck. It was a warm, companionable embrace that she returned by wrapping her own arm around his waist. Always stiff and uncertain with people who touched without reservation, it seemed incredibly natural to return Toby's undemanding affection, and the only feelings it aroused in Jessie were ones of easy friendship. Still, it was totally out of character for her, and she marked the event with a small quiver of pleasure that she could respond so easily. It was as if her feelings for Haveron had opened a reservoir of warmth open to anyone else who cared to enter. It was the first step out of the self-imposed isolation she had practised all her life, and suddenly she liked very much the woman she was becoming.

Toby cradled her face in both big hands and pecked her lightly on the nose before climbing into the truck, and Jessie smiled happily as he drove away.

Haveron, invisible in his immobility just a short distance away at the top of the ridge, did not smile at all.

CHAPTER TWELVE

HAVERON'S attitude over the next few weeks was almost manic with abrupt changes, and Jessie found herself alternately miserable and content in direct relation to his moods. At times he would look at her with such wistful longing that she would be tempted to throw herself into his arms; but then his expression would alter slightly, and he would eye her with a cold indifference that made her back off mentally in confusion, wondering if the man had any human feelings at all. Eventually his mood settled into a constant, cool aloofness, and Jessie began to wonder if that one night of passion at the lodge had only been a dream.

He had returned to the lodge after that first night at the cabin, saying simply that he had business there which required his attention, assuring her that Ice Cream no longer needed frequent night-time checks. But late that night Jessie had awakened and peered out of her bedroom window to see Haveron crouched over the doe with a flashlight. Apparently he thought she needed attention enough to merit the long walk to and from the lodge, and Jessie crawled silently back into bed, wondering what she had done to drive him away.

Although he appeared at the cabin at least three times a day to minister to the deer, his visits were short, and any attempt Jessie made at conversation was quickly stifled by his curt, monosyllabic answers.

'What's wrong with you?' she had demanded desperately after two weeks of such treatment, not caring any more that the question exposed her vulnerability. 'What on earth did I do to make you back off so quickly?'

'Back off from what?' he had asked coldly, and she had retreated to the cabin, mortified by the rebuff.

From what, indeed? she asked herself furiously once she was out of his sight. A few moments of passion that you thought promised more? How naïve, how stupid you were! But even as it faded from her memory, that one, fragile connection with Haveron lingered as a mutual, almost magical coming together, and she could hardly believe it was gone.

Without conscious intention, she soon matched his attitude, frost for frost, and the days melted into weeks of stiff, formal exchanges that centred totally around Ice Cream. She was the only common ground they had now.

It was only during Toby's periodic visits that Jessie felt human herself, as they engaged in the easy give-and-take of a normal relationship between friends. She never spoke of her relationship with Haveron and, wisely, Toby never asked about it. It was enough that he came, full of laughter and anecdotes about the villagers, relieving for the length of his stays the terrible tension she felt in Haveron's company.

It was a morning in late October when Jessie crawled out of bed, suddenly aware that the seasons had changed when she hadn't been looking. Frost lay heavily on the dried, wrinkled ferns that had once carpeted the forest floor with the rich green of life, and the invincible white pines seemed oddly stiff, as if bracing themselves for the onslaught of winter.

She wiggled her fingers out of the window at the doe who stood placidly in the early morning cold, a stalk of hay stuck comically in the thick fuzz of one velvet ear. 'Hungry, are you?' Jessie murmured into the glass of the frosty window, and Ice Cream stamped one delicate forefoot as if in answer to the question she couldn't possibly have heard.

Jessie smiled to herself as she pulled on long johns, heavy corduroy slacks, a T-shirt, and then a huge, brown, bulky-knit sweater. No matter how miserable Haveron's inexplicable coldness made her, Ice Cream still had the power to pull her temporarily out of her depression.

She shrugged into a heavy parka, stepped into fur-lined boots, then went into the kitchen to fill a bucket from the bag of grain stored in the pantry. She paused for a moment, letting the smooth, golden kernels run through her fingers, remembering the last time she had seen Haveron, over a week before. He had carried in this very bag of grain to replace the empty one, dropping it on the pantry floorboards with a heavy thud.

'I'll bring down three more of these when I have time,' he'd said brusquely. 'That should take her through the winter, providing she stays that long.'

'What about hay?'

'I'll still have to bring that one bale at a time, about every three days. Otherwise she'd gorge herself. Besides that, a hay stack would attract more deer than you could handle.'

'That's a lot of trips. Seems like too much trouble.'

'Not at all. And don't worry. I won't bother you when I come. You'll never even know I'm here.'

Jessie closed her eyes at the painful recollection, thinking he could not have been more clear about not wanting to see her. 'Stay inside,' he seemed to be saying. 'I'll drop off the hay and then leave, and we'll never even have to meet.'

A rapid clatter on the front porch startled her out of her reverie. 'Tap dancing again?' she said with a smile as she pulled open the front door. Ice Cream answered with that peculiar impatient bleat she reserved for meal time. Jessie scooted past her down the steps, laughing as the doe scrambled after her with hooves slipping on the smooth boards; then she set the bucket down on the ground.

While the doe buried her muzzle in the grain, Jessie took her customary seat on the porch steps and dropped her chin into her hands, immeasurably content simply to watch. The hourly feedings of mash that first week; the endless trips with water buckets; the constant dressing of the once ghastly wound—all had paid off a thousandfold. In spite of the coolness between them, she and Haveron had at least shared in the wonder of gaining this wild creature's trust, and the rewards were countless. Still playful with the antics of a young doe just approaching maturity, Ice Cream had surprised them more than once with bucking leaps of pure joy as her recovery progressed. At those times, at least, they had laughed together. And though Haveron had warned her time and again that the doe would simply be gone one morning, returned to the wilds that owned her, the time had not come yet. Jessie was grateful for every morning she found the doe on the front porch, and refused to anticipate the crushing loneliness that would settle over her life once Ice Cream was gone.

'You're too attached to her!' Haveron blurted out one day, his eyes unusually dark as he watched the doe nuzzle at Jessie's hair. 'It's going to end, you know.'

Jessie had looked up at him with mild surprise. 'Everything does,' she said simply. 'At least I've had it for this long; longer than anything else in my life.'

It had been long enough for half-a-dozen paintings and a hundred sketches; and while Jessie's art had always been extraordinary, these were breathtaking. Ice Cream looked out from the canvas with those large, polished eyes as if a puff of air would breathe life into the two-dimensional painting, and its subject would simply bound away. Every nuance of colour was perfect, every stroke of the brush tenderly placed; and if her previous work had been the realisation of great talent, then these were the realisations of great love. Two of the canvases were ready for shipment to the magazine, easily fulfilling the basic requirement that each work should depict a deer in its natural environment; but Jessie had not wrapped them yet. She was waiting for something; and in that deep, unspoken part of her mind, she knew she wanted Haveron to see them first.

Ice Cream licked the last of the grain from the bucket, then butted it on to its side, bleating her disgust.

'No more, you clown,' Jessie said, walking over to stroke the lifted head. 'Now you stay put. I'll get you some water.'

By the time she walked back out on to the porch, water sloshing over the rim of the filled bucket, Haveron was kneeling in front of the doe, submitting meekly to the inquisitive muzzle that searched his pockets for the expected carrot.

Jessie stopped where she stood, trying to slow the insistent clamour of a heart that had yet to learn this man was no longer interested. 'Good morning,' she said breathlessly, cherishing the sound of those simple words, just because they were the first she had spoken to him in so many days.

'Good morning,' he answered, and Jessie followed the frosty cloud of his breath with her eyes, suddenly chilled by the visual reminder of the temperature. 'I never expect her to be here,' he said. 'I keep thinking that the next time I stop, the yard will be empty.'

He offered a carrot in his open palm, then laughed when the doe butted his stomach, begging for more.

'Will you have coffee?' Jessie asked timidly, steeling herself for another cold refusal.

'Aren't you busy?'

'Of course not, although I have been,' she answered, thinking of all those lonely hours in front of her drawing board.

'I'm well aware of that,' he said stiffly, making her wonder if he'd been peeking through the windows, watching her work. 'Well, why not? I have time this morning.'

She led the way into the cabin, leaving him in the living-room while she went to start the coffee maker, ridiculously happy just to have him in the same house.

'Hey!' he called from the other room. 'Haven't you brought in any more wood yet? The first storm is on its way in, and you're going to be caught without. . .'

Then his voice stopped abruptly, and Jessie cocked her head in the kitchen, waiting for the chastisement to continue. After a long moment of absolute silence, she crept out to the living-room to see what had stopped the harsh rebuke.

Haveron stood with his back towards her, facing the first painting she'd done of Ice Cream, his shoulders strangely slumped, his head bent. She walked quietly over to stand next to him, looking down at the painting, and then up at his face.

'My God,' he said softly. 'When did you do this?'

'Before I did this,' she answered, lifting the cover from another canvas that was propped up against the wall. 'And this, and this.' She removed the protective sheets from every painting of the doe, all lined up against the length of the wall like a classroom exhibit; and then she stood back and waited anxiously for him to speak, but he only stared at them, one by one, and said nothing.

'Well?' she prompted finally, and nearly crumpled to see the desperation in the eyes he turned towards her.

'I'll buy them,' he said stonily, his tone a direct contradiction to the longing in his eyes. 'Every one.'

'Buy them?' she asked weakly. She didn't know what she had expected him to say, but it certainly hadn't been that. 'Whatever for?'

He turned back to face the first canvas, the muscle in his jaw tight. His words were clipped brutally, as if they were being extracted against his will. 'I just want them, that's all.'

'Well, they're not for sale,' she said almost spitefully. He had taken something she wanted away from her; now suddenly she had the same power over him.

'I can meet your price,' he said stiffly, 'whatever it is. I won't even dicker.'

'My price is knowing why you want them so badly,' she said.

'You want praise?' he asked with contempt. 'Fine. I wouldn't have thought you would need it, but I'm willing to meet those terms. They're excellent. Perhaps the best wildlife paintings I've ever seen. I'd be a fool not to acquire as many as I could before you become too well known, and the prices become ridiculous.'

'And that's it?'

'What better reason could there be? Oh, I admit I have a certain fondness for the subject. I wouldn't mind having a reminder of Ice Cream—God! That's a stupid name!—for when she's gone.'

'You could take a picture,' Jessie said flatly.

'No,' he said, and suddenly his voice was softer, warmer. 'No, Jess. A photograph wouldn't be the same. There wouldn't be any of you in it.'

Jessie's mouth dropped open in the same instant that Haveron stiffened, as if realising he had confessed far too much. He slammed the door behind him as he made an abrupt exit, before Jessie could find the words she wanted to say. By the time she found her legs to rush after him, he was over the ridge on his way back to the lodge.

She stood alone in the middle of the empty trail, staring mindlessly at where Haveron had been just a moment before, stunned by the enormity of the quantum leap she was now considering. A step forward represented a milestone; an unmistakable surrender to her need for another human being. Returning to the cabin meant returning to total independence—to the Jessie Loren she had always been. She took a deep breath, pulled the parka more closely round her, flipped up the fur-lined hood, and began her very first dogged pursuit of a man.

She almost giggled, striding between the frosty pines on her way to the lodge. Objectively speaking, what she was doing was preposterous. He had said only a few words—faint encouragement of the most ambiguous kind—and yet here she was, ready to bet the whole of her pride and the rest of her life on the slim chance that he had meant much more. She was chasing him, tracking him down; as earnest in the hunt as any predator had ever been, stalking its prey. Mother would never believe it, she thought, smiling. Walt would never believe it. No one who had known her would believe she was capable of traipsing off through a frozen forest in pursuit of a man who had exhibited nothing but cool indifference for such a long time now.

But they don't know Haveron like I do, she told herself. They don't understand how afraid he is to trust, to ever rely on and become attached to another human being. Only I can understand that, because I've lived that same empty existence myself. But one of us has to stop being afraid.

She slipped through the front door of the lodge without knocking, and called out his name as she removed her boots and parka. There was no answering call, but her courage held. She felt stronger, and happier, and more sure of herself than she had in weeks.

A little wall mirror caught her attention with its reflection of a woman who looked only vaguely familiar. Long brown hair swirled around her shoulders in a cloud that was totally uncontrolled, and totally alive. The matching brown eyes were enormous in the tiny face flushed with cold, unnaturally bright and optimistic. The small mouth was opened in a wondering smile, and Jessie reached up with one finger to touch the corner of the curving lips, not quite believing they were real.

'How about that,' she whispered to the mirror, almost mesmerised by her own reflection. 'You are pretty, at that.'

Then she turned and called out his name again; and still there was no answer. The lodge was empty. She checked every room upstairs, and most of the rooms on the main floor before she finally admitted to herself that he was not in the building. Now that she thought of it, that was typical. He was no doubt out wandering through the woods, agonising over emotions he could control no better than she could control hers; trying to find solace in the wilderness that was so much a part of him.

It didn't really matter. He would return eventually, and Jessie was prepared to wait. She had come too far now to turn back.

She fidgeted impatiently in a lobby chair for a while, then wandered out to the enormous kitchen to start a pot of coffee. While waiting for the interminable brew cycle to finish, she sat on a stool at one of the butcher-block tables, drumming her fingers on the smooth surface. The lodge was filled with that heavy, ominous silence common to very large houses when the occupants are absent. Her thoughts seemed magnified by the stillness, as if every one were shouted aloud.

What are you waiting for? that old sensible part of her mind prodded. What will you say when he comes back? That you love him? That you're prepared to track him over half the upper peninsula if necessary? That there's no limit to how great a fool of yourself you're prepared to make?

She blushed as she sat there, knowing perfectly well that given the chance she could convince herself that she was wasting her time, and that Haveron's comment had simply been poorly phrased, and misinterpreted by her. What was it he had said? That a photograph of Ice Cream wouldn't be the same as the painting, because it wouldn't have any of her in it? Were those the words that had sent her after him with her heart fluttering and her hopes high? Just those? Why, he could simply have meant that he admired her artistic talent. It might just have been impersonal praise for her skill. *She* was the one who gave those few words all that heavy, personal meaning.

'Oh dear,' she whispered to the empty room, completely convinced now that this was indeed the case, and that she was on the greatest fool's errand of all time.

She slid quickly from the stool with only one thought in mind: escaping back to the cabin before she could be discovered in her near-folly. His voice stopped her before she had even reached the kitchen doorway.

'You have a real talent for trespassing, don't you?'

She jumped and spun where she stood, her heart hammering. 'Where did you come from?'

'I was walking. I came in the side door, and followed the smell of coffee out here.'

Jessie stood as if rooted to the spot, her mind racing, trying to formulate a believable reason for her presence here.

'Why did you follow me?' he demanded.

She turned her head away. 'It's a little hard to explain.'

'Try.'

She looked to his face for the smallest sign of warmth, and finding none, said simply, 'Because I'm more of a fool than I ever thought I could be, I guess. And now I think I should be going.'

'What?' His smile was cold and unpleasant. 'Before you've had coffee? Now that's a shame, and after all the trouble you took to make it, too.' His voice dropped lower and lower down the scale, rich with sarcasm, yet the effect was the same as if he had been shouting. 'Why don't you admit the truth? That you can't stay away from the lodge, that you still think of it as home, but you just can't stand being here when I am?'

'What?' she whispered in disbelief, now totally confused. 'But that's not true. I was following you, not trying to avoid you!'

'Really? Well, if that's the case, how do you explain rushing away the moment I return? What's the matter? Did you forget you were expecting company today?'

'Company?' she echoed in a small voice, shaking her head in confusion, bewildered as much by the tightly controlled anger in his voice as she was by his words. 'What are you talking about? The only company I ever have is Toby, and. . .' She stopped in mid-sentence, alarmed by the sudden tightening of his jaw at the mention of Toby's name. 'Do you know Toby?' she whispered, wondering what festering wound lay between the two men.

'Only by sight,' he snapped. 'But you seem to know him very well. You see him often enough. So why don't you tell me about him? Tell me all about your good friend Toby.'

There was a peculiar challenge to his contempt, as if he were daring her to speak; and suddenly she had the sickening feeling that he knew something she didn't. Something horrible about Toby. Her thoughts fluttered through all the possible things one could do to incur Haveron's wrath, and kept returning to the only crime she knew he wouldn't forgive. Dear Lord. He thought Toby was the poacher, although she knew that was impossible. She could hardly imagine that gentle, soft-spoken giant harming anything.

'No,' she said sharply, shaking her head in strong denial. 'I know what you're thinking, and you're wrong. I *know* Toby. He was the one who brought me out here from the station, my very first day, and he's never been anything but kind. He's a good, decent man, who takes the trouble to look in on me even when it takes time away from his own girl, and he loves Ice Cream. Now does that sound like a poacher to you?'

She could barely see through the haze of indignation that had sent her words tumbling faster and faster until now she was breathing hard with the effort. 'You're wrong about him, Haveron. Absolutely wrong. He doesn't even hunt *in* season, let alone out of it.'

She glared at him defiantly, her face set, until finally she realised his expression was no longer rigid with suspicion, but only faintly quizzical.

'I never thought he was a poacher, Jessie,' he said softly.

'Well what, then?' she demanded, ready to defend the man who had befriended her against all accusations.

His words were so quietly spoken that she had to cock her head to hear him. 'I thought he was your lover.'

There was no need for an astonished denial. He could see it in her face. And there was something else, too: a slow flood of relief as she put all the pieces together; then a bright, hard expression of exultant disbelief. 'I don't believe it,' she whispered, inching closer to him, drinking in the sudden warmth in his eyes, the easy, relaxed curve of lips drawing into a sheepish smile. 'You mean all this time . . . all the coldness, all the indifference . . . all that was because. . .' She stopped within a foot of where he stood and looked up at him with wonder.

He touched her cheek gently with one hand and nodded. 'Disgusting, isn't it? Such a basic, human emotion. I always thought I was above that sort of thing.' Then he shrugged. 'I was jealous, Jess. It's as simple as that.'

He was smiling down at her now, but she saw the pain of memory in his eyes. 'I thought we had something that night at the lodge; something unbelievably special. And then the next day I saw you with Toby, and everything fell apart. It was as if the night before had all been on my side, or just in my imagination; and I decided it had only been another fling for a city-wise person like you.' He closed his eyes briefly and shook his head. 'I nearly went crazy. I tried to stay away, Jess, but I couldn't. And whenever I saw that truck parked at the cabin, the knife went a little deeper, and still I couldn't stay away. I went on torturing myself, coming down every day, just to be near you, just to see you, even when you didn't know I was there.'

His hand slid from her cheek to rest lightly on her shoulder, his thumb massaging a slow circle in the hollow of her neck. She wanted to comfort him, wanted to erase the memory of all that senseless suffering from his face; but she couldn't speak, not with his hand on her shoulder like that. She couldn't even move, though she wanted nothing more than to throw herself into his arms. She could only stand there, helplessly immobile, staring up into his eyes, as if she were frozen in a moment of time she would never be able to escape.

He dropped his chin to gaze down at her, himself a victim of the same paralysis that held her, flooding her eyes with a tide of dammed emotion that had been held in check too long.

He feels what I feel, she thought with wonder; and a rush of gratitude that such incredible sensations could actually be shared with another person washed over her.

She became aware that her own breathing had quickened only when she noticed that his had, too. They were still a foot apart, and yet it felt as if they were already joined, united by an invisible thread every bit as strong as the passion that now controlled them both. He held her with his eyes as surely as if her head were in a vice, unable to turn away; and still he didn't touch her, save for the hand resting quietly on her shoulder, as calm and removed from the feelings that flared between them as if it had belonged to someone else. In a distant, instinctive part of her mind, Jessie knew that if his lips descended to hers, if just one more part of his body touched hers, something inside would explode, and her knees would buckle beneath her. And when his head finally lowered slowly, narrowing the space between them in an agonisingly slow measure of seconds, when she finally felt the hot rush of his breath on her face, she was not surprised to hear the small cry of release that escaped her own lips just before his mouth crashed against hers. Her knees did buckle, and she sagged against him like a boneless puppet, oblivious to the bruising urgency of his mouth, now feeling only the exquisitely painful pressure of his chest flattening her swollen breasts. She felt the consuming drive of a passion she never knew she possessed racing through her body with a fiery heat, demanding fulfilment as she ground her hips wantonly against his, gasping at the pressure of his own desire, smiling when an agonised moan escaped his lips. Jessie felt a sharp, peculiarly feminine stab of satisfaction to know she had brought him to this; that she had levelled the fearsome Haveron to this very human plane. There was no superior force in the tangled line of their two bodies pressing together. They were gripped equally by the magnitude of a desire that made them identically weak in the face of it, and identically strong.

He had both arms round her now, his fingers splayed out against her back, pulling her into him. When had that happened? And when had her own arms wrapped round his neck, tangling her fingers in his hair, pulling his head down towards hers? She only knew that now he was pulling away, grasping her by the shoulders as if to hold her off, his head bent, his hair quivering with the ragged gasps of his breathing. He lifted his head and smiled weakly, sheepishly, his eyes acknowledging the promise of what was to come.

'I want it to be right,' he said hoarsely. 'I want you to know who and what I am first, and then come to me willingly. No more secrets. No more things unsaid, or unknown. I want this forever. Do you understand?'

She nodded wordlessly, looking up into his eyes, licking once at her swollen lips, emitting a soft cry when he bent quickly to touch her mouth with his tongue. He shuddered at her cry, then turned quickly from her, closing his eyes as an indication of what toll this gesture extracted.

'Now come with me,' he said, taking her hand, leading her across the kitchen to the double doors that Jessie remembered led to the games room. She stumbled once on legs oddly weak, and wondered dimly what could possibly be of interest in a room filled with billiard tables.

Jessie caught her breath when she entered the long, narrow room, simply because it was the only place in the lodge that did not look exactly as she remembered it from twenty years before. Haveron had been so meticulous about preserving the past in every other room that the transformation of this one surprised her.

The full length of the west wall was still banked with floor to ceiling windows that looked out over the forest as it rolled away down to Loren Lake, but the view was the only thing that seemed even remotely familiar.

'What is all this, Haveron?' Her eyes darted from a series of computer terminals arranged along one wall to the papers and charts scattered across various tables, and then to an enormous desk that supported a complex array of electronic equipment. Finally her gaze came to astonished rest upon the one pool table that still remained in the room, with its side pockets the only visible reminder of the table's original purpose. Its top had been transformed into a topographical model of some sort, complete with toy-sized buildings scattered randomly among the tiny replicas of densely wooded hills. 'What is it?' she repeated, walking over to touch the tiny trees carefully with one finger.

'It's Loren Resort,' he smiled; and then, in answer to her quick glance of puzzlement, 'or what it will be, by next year.'

Jessie leaned over the table, recognising now the irregular, flat blue oblong that obviously represented Loren Lake, and the rise next to it that must be Hunter's Ridge. But the rest was unfamiliar. There were several interconnecting trails carved throughout the model; trails she knew did not exist. And although the scene clearly reflected the lodge and the present cabins, including her own, there were several others scattered about at junctions of the tiny trails. 'What are all these little buildings,' she pointed in confusion, 'and these little lines? Are they trails? And what about those little blocks sitting on the lake? What are they supposed to be?'

He laughed at the rapid-fire flood of questions, and chose to answer the last one. 'Those are ice fishing houses,' he said. 'I've been stocking the lake for four years now, with northern, bass, and even muskie. There's every fish an ice fisherman ever dreamed of out there, and in great plenty.'

He moved next to her at the table, caught up in the enthusiasm of describing the model, as if she were a potential investor. 'And all these are cross-country ski trails, hiking trails in the summer. There will be over one hundred miles of them, all told; through every kind of terrain imaginable, past all the salt licks and watering places I already showed you. And these are extra cabins, totally isolated from the lodge for those who really want a week in the wilderness, but all connected by phone in case of emergency.' He continued his explanation, punctuating it with gestures, his brow furrowed earnestly as he laid out his dream. Finally he finished, leaning back against the table with his arms crossed over his chest, his eyes watching her carefully. 'It's the resort, Jess, just like it used to be, only better. And this time people won't come here to kill the wildlife; they'll come to watch it, to learn from it, to become a part of nature, instead of taking part of nature away.'

So this was the little boy's dream, she thought, staring at the model with a wondering smile. Vengeance had not prompted his return to this place. He had not come back to close off the land, to punish the townspeople who had treated him so badly in his youth; in fact, the townspeople had nothing to do with this project. He had come back to the only friends he had ever known, the wild creatures who had once been his only companions; and now he was creating a refuge for them, one that could be shared with the world.

'Haveron,' she whispered, 'why didn't you tell me? Why didn't you show this to me before?'

He looked down and pursed his lips. 'I almost did . . . that first night . . . but then things seemed to get out of hand. I'm fighting some pretty powerful lobbyists in the state legislature, trying to get the land round the resort declared a wildlife refuge. It's an absolutely essential part of this project. I can't afford to have hunters packing long-range rifles just the other side of my property lines. It wouldn't be safe for the guests. And if the people in this county knew I was trying to restrict hunting even further, they'd add their voices to those already opposing me. It just might be enough to tip the scales in their favour. . .'

Jessie closed her eyes. 'And you thought I'd spread word of your plans so that the townspeople could organise against you.'

'I didn't know,' he whispered. 'I just didn't know. After all, your family made a living from hunters. I couldn't expect you to understand, only. . .'

'Only what?'

He sighed and smiled. 'Only when I saw you sketching the buck that morning, there was something . . .' he frowned, searching for the proper words, '. . . something almost reverent in your drawing; something that made me think maybe, just maybe, you felt the same way I did about the wilderness, and the wildlife.' He shrugged helplessly and looked away.

Jessie reached out tentatively to touch his arm. It almost seemed too good to be true, that she could just reach out and touch him whenever she wanted to, and she felt a little tremor snake up through her arm when she felt the coarse knit of his sweater beneath her fingertips. 'And what's all the rest of this for?' she asked quietly, nodding towards the computers.

'Oh, that,' he answered casually, as if it were totally irrelevant. 'Those are computer links with my offices in New York, Denver, Seattle . . . that sort of thing.'

She chuckled in amazement, then followed him back to the kitchen, shaking her head at all she had learned about this man in the last few moments. When he put a mug of coffee in her hand, she looked straight into eyes that held the expectant, childlike pride of a little boy.

'So Ron Michels made good,' she understated, grinning.

'I suppose so,' he shrugged, almost embarrassed.

'And what do you do in all these offices of yours, Haveron?'

'Oil investments, mostly.' He took a careful sip from his mug. 'I bought a little piece of land in Alaska with the money I'd saved while I worked on the ore boats.'

He shook his head, smiling at the memory. 'I had intended to build a little cabin and hide there for the rest of my life, but my little cabin ended up sitting on one of the most lucrative oil deposits in the state; and before I knew it I had lots and lots of money, but no place to hang my hat. So I started shopping for another piece of wilderness I could call my own; only a bigger one this time, since I had more money to play with.'

'And?'

'And I bought Candervas Canyon, in Colorado. Heard of it?'

Jessie's mouth formed a silent whistle. Candervas Canyon was known nationwide as a naturalist's paradise, nestled in the wilds of the Rocky Mountain foothills. Thousands of acres had been converted into a combination refuge and resort, attracting nature-lovers from all over the states. 'You did that?' she whispered.

He just nodded.

'But, Haveron, I don't understand. Candervas Canyon is one of the wealthiest tourist attractions in the West. If that's what you're going to do here, the town's economy will boom. They couldn't possibly object!'

'Really?' His brows lifted sceptically. 'How many people up here have even heard of Candervas Canyon? All they'd understand was that I was trying to reduce hunter traffic even more, and that's the only kind of tourist they believe in.'

'You're not giving them enough credit, or yourself,' she frowned. 'You could explain it to them, you could. . .'

'Oh, come off it, Jess,' he interrupted her gently. 'You know these people as well as I do. Their whole lives are wrapped up in that old, macho image of man against the wild. It isn't just the money. It goes a lot deeper than that. Some of these men *need* to stalk and kill. It fits their image of a man's man.'

Jessie frowned and caught her lower lip between her teeth, considering. He was right, of course. There were still a lot of men who responded to the age-old instinct that made men hunters, especially up here, and those were the ones who would be most vocal, most adamantly opposed to Haveron's resort, even though it promised plenty to the community as a whole. 'But they'll thank you eventually,' she offered hopefully.

'Only after the fact. After they find jobs with the resort and see their town come alive again. After all that, maybe they'll thank me, although personally I couldn't care less. But until then they'll fight me every step of the way.' He set his empty mug down forcefully on the counter, and reached for the coffee pot.

'When was the last time you trusted anyone, Haveron?' she asked gently, and he raised his head to look directly at her.

'There never was a last time. This is the first.'

'It's a beautiful dream, Haveron, and everyone stands to gain. You'll benefit, the town will benefit, the wildlife will benefit—I'd never do anything to jeopardise that. I won't mention your plans to anyone.'

He closed his eyes briefly and nodded once, and although the gesture was a simple one, Jessie recognised the import of that moment. She had just received a part of Haveron that had never been given away before.

She had not heard the blaring harshness of a telephone's ring for such a long time that when the sound came from the games room she jumped in surprise. Haveron smiled at her reaction and bent to kiss her lightly on the top of her head before leaving to answer the phone. 'Don't go anywhere,' he whispered into her ear. 'This day is just beginning.'

She shivered at the promise in his words, instantly forgetting the plans for the resort along with the first twenty-eight years of her life. She would mark time now from the moment he walked back into the room, when everything would begin.

In a few moments he returned, wearing a small, frustrated smile of disappointment. He slipped quickly into the coat he had tossed on the chair earlier, and gestured with his head towards the front door. 'We have to go, Jess. That was the emergency weather service chain call. Apparently we're in for it. Blizzard warnings for the next twenty-four hours, with over two feet of snow predicted and forty-mile-an-hour winds. That means total isolation up here. We've got a couple of hours to get ready for this one, and not much more.'

Jessie felt the quiver of little-girl excitement at the prospect of her first snow in nearly twenty years, and Haveron saw the anticipation on her face and chuckled.

'I can see by your expression that you've forgotten how bad it can be. I hope you still feel that way after we've been snowed in for a few days. Now come on.'

He led the way to the front door and held her coat as she shrugged into it. She turned and looked up at his face, marvelling at how very kind he could look without tension stiffening his features. 'Will I be snowed in with you?' she asked, smiling.

'Yes,' he whispered, bending his head towards hers, his eyes narrowing. Then he stopped and closed his eyes with a resigned smile. 'Jessie, if I touch you now, I'll never be able to stop.' He straightened reluctantly and zipped up his parka like a barrier between them. 'I have to make a trip into town first. We'll need some emergency supplies I just hadn't thought to pick up yet; kerosene for the lamps, especially. I doubt if the power at the cabin will last through the night.'

'We'll stay at the cabin?'

He nodded, smiling. 'I don't think we have a choice, do we? Ice Cream is there.'

'Haveron,' she whispered, reaching for him, 'I want to say it now. I want everything to be said now.'

He forced her hands back to her sides with a pained smiled, then touched his forefinger to her lips to silence her. 'We have time,' he said softly. 'It's going to be a long, long winter.'

CHAPTER THIRTEEN

THERE was an ominous quality to the hush of the forest that Haveron and Jessie both sensed the moment they walked outside. The woods seemed more like a painted backdrop for a drama yet to come than the cradle of life they knew it to be. There was no busy chattering of birds, no scurrying sounds of life, no motion whatsoever. The world seemed suspended in one collectively held breath, and the silence of waiting was unnatural.

The brittle crunch of frozen leaves under their feet shattered the stillness like the crack of a gunshot. Jessie shivered from more than the cold as she waited for Haveron to bring his truck round from the lodge garage. The muted roar of its powerful engine seemed a dangerous violation of the silence, as if its very sound would lead the coming storm directly to them.

Even Ice Cream was strangely subdued as they pulled up next to the cabin, responding to the sixth sense that warns animals to conserve energy and heat for an upcoming trial of endurance. She stood motionless by the front porch as the truck ground to a halt, her head lowered, her eyes watchful.

Jessie's teeth chattered a little, and Haveron reached over to warm her cheek with one hand. 'Check the food supply while I'm gone,' he told her. 'Anything you're short of I can collect from the lodge when I get back. And you might dig out the kerosene lamps, and spread some straw for the doe under the overhang on the east side of the cabin.' He paused to chuckle. 'You know, I still can't bring myself to call her by that ridiculous name.' He smiled at Jessie's affected expression of insult, then he was all business again. 'I'll start bringing in some deadwood when everything else is taken care of. There's enough close to the cabin to keep the fireplace blazing for a few days at least, and I get the feeling we're going to need it.'

'We may not need as much as you think,' she smiled, climbing down from the cab. 'Don't be long.'

She watched the truck rumble away until she could no longer see the frosty plumes of its exhaust, then she hugged herself with both arms, containing a shiver. Already it seemed colder, and the silence was even more oppressive with Haveron gone.

Ice Cream walked slowly over to stand next to her, butting her nose against Jessie's side until she received the expected caress. Jessie sensed the doe's instinctive need for the closeness of another being in an environment that seemed suddenly sinister. She felt exactly the same way herself. She wondered if all living creatures sought security in numbers in the face of a coming storm.

'Poor Ice Cream,' she cooed, kneeling to rock the elegant head gently in both hands. 'You'll be all alone out here tonight, but don't worry. If it gets too bad, we'll simply bring you inside.'

The doe blinked a mute reponse, then emitted a comical bleat directly into Jessie's face.

'Come on, you clown. Let's get your bed ready.'

Jessie laid a thick bed of yellow straw next to the cabin's east wall, then dragged a new bale of hay over to the improvised shelter. Ice Cream stepped directly into the centre of what was to be her refuge for the night, then snatched a few wisps of hay from the bale as if to take possession. Her tiny hooves sank deep into the thick layer of straw, and even though Jessie knew that the hollow the doe would create when she lay down would provide some protection, she worried that it wouldn't be enough.

'Ah, well,' she sighed, straightening from her labours, pressing her gloved hands to the small of her back. 'It's the best we can do, I'm afraid, short of building you a house of your own; and Haveron says you wouldn't like that anyway.' She rubbed the top of the doe's head affectionately, then left her to start gathering deadwood to pile on the porch. There was no need for Haveron to do all the work, and it was something she should have done weeks ago anyway. Besides, the more she could do while he was gone meant the more time they would have together when he returned.

There was a sizeable, jumbled stack of wood cluttering the front porch by the time she heard the faint reverberations of his engine threading up through the trees from the highway. She smiled involuntarily at the sound, anticipating the sight of him as if she were a child awaiting Christmas. A worrisome, uncharacteristic concern about her appearance flashed through her mind, and when she recognised it for what it was, she laughed out loud in sheer pleasure. She was exhibiting all the symptoms of a young girl in love, anticipating her first date with the man of her dreams. She had always looked on such feelings as frivolous from her lofty, serious perch far removed from the normal range of a young girl's experience; but they didn't seem frivolous now. At twenty-eight years old, she was a young girl in love for the very first time, and she looked it.

She felt strangely uplifted as the heavy four-wheel-drive truck pulled to a stop in front of the cabin. It felt as if every part of her body was connected by strings to some control centre far above her, and the puppet master was pulling the strings gently, lifting her lips, her eyes, her heart; transforming her physical being into the embodiment of a great, universal smile. She had never felt such joy, never imagined its existence; and she refused to believe that anyone else had ever felt it before her. Her dark eyes glowed and sparkled with warmth, flashing against the icy rose of flushed cheeks. She pushed her parka's hood back impatiently, freeing her long hair to lift in the cool caress of a sudden breeze.

She watched Haveron open the truck door, step out, lean across the seat to gather two heavyweight bags;

then straighten and nudge the door closed with his knee, all the while keeping his back towards her. Even his heavy parka could not completely disguise the purely masculine grace of his well-muscled body, and her heart contracted to look at him, even as her smile broadened.

The smile faltered after a moment, and her brows twitched. Why didn't he turn round? Why was he just standing there, his back towards her, not moving? The only indication of life was the frost of his breath rising above his head. Except for that, he might well have been a lifeless statue, planted in that spot forever.

Suddenly Jessie felt the icy grip of foreboding close round her heart. 'Haveron?' she whispered, one hand tentatively lifted, her voice tiny and lost in the vastness of that moment. And then her lips formed his name once again, but no sound came out of her mouth.

She would remember his turn forever as an execution of slow motion. Endless seconds ticked away from the moment his body started to rotate until it completed its turn. And then she looked upon his face and the world went suddenly mad, toppling her into a spinning vortex of nightmarish confusion where nothing made sense. His expression was black with hatred, and his eyes directed that hatred towards her.

His dark hair was tousled, crashing over his forehead as if it had already done battle with itself; his eyes were so darkly green that they looked almost black; his mouth was a slash of control in a face pale beneath its naturally dark complexion. Jessie stumbled backward one step, then two, her lips and eyes forming three circles of alarm.

'What is it?' she whispered, unconsciously tugging her parka more closely around her. 'What's wrong?' She felt the straining ache of leg muscles instinctively poised to flee, and for one brief moment she felt the childish impulse simply to sag to the ground and cry. 'Dammit!' she shouted, meeting the awful condemnation in his eyes. 'Tell me what's wrong!'

He pressed his lips together even more firmly, as though he knew that speech would tap the awesome force of his pent-up rage, and once released he would be unable to control it. His only response was a tightening of his arms around the bags he held, a flashing dagger of hate from his eyes that pierced her where she stood, then he stalked past her up the steps, into the cabin, saying nothing.

Jessie followed him cautiously, her stomach churning, her startled heart beating a rapid, shallow tattoo against her chest. She closed the door behind her and leaned against it, as much to prop her shaky knees upright as to block his exit.

He set the bags down on an end table with exaggerated care, although nothing inside them was nearly as fragile as the woman who waited breathlessly for him to speak. Then he turned to face her, taking several deep breaths to bring his voice under control before speaking. Jessie noticed that he did not look directly at her now, as though the sight of her was too distasteful to be borne. When the words finally rolled out of his mouth with the muted rumble of distant thunder, she felt the first overwhelming sense of hopelessness.

'Who is buying your calendar paintings?'

The question seemed so irrelevant, so totally dissociated from the current situation that she couldn't imagine his reason for asking it.

'A magazine,' she answered helplessly. 'It's called *The Wild Life*. Why?'

'You knew that?' The question was obviously an appalled accusation, and she shook her head in confusion, shrugging with her palms held up in mystified supplication.

'Of course I knew that. I signed a contract with them. Haveron, what's this all about? I don't understand what. . .'

His smile silenced her instantly. It was far more frightening than any outburst would have been. 'It's about trust, Jessie. That's what it's about,' he replied with deadly calm, still refusing to look directly at her, still wearing that cold, sickly smile. 'You're quite a heroine in town, you know. They can't say enough about you; about how you'll single-handedly save this area from a slow demise. You're the best thing that's happened to them in years.'

'What?' she whispered weakly, now more confused than ever.

'Excellent!' He applauded her with two loud, measured claps of his hands. 'Your confusion is almost believable.'

'Haveron, stop it!' she shouted, rushing over to grab desperately at his arm.

He snatched her hand and flung it from him with an expression of genuine loathing. 'Don't pretend any more!' he hissed, looking right at her now, frightening her with his eyes. 'The whole town is humming about that calendar, and we know exactly what kind of product *The Wild Life* puts out, don't we? Twelve beautiful scenes of game animals in their natural environments, complete with captions that tell precisely where those animals can be found. It's a treasure map for hunters, isn't it? No wonder you weren't worried about my resort plans limiting the hunting traffic. Your calendar will bring more hunters to this area in one year than it's ever seen before, and that kind of economic surge will certainly quash any proposals for a wildlife refuge!'

Jessie's mouth fell open and she locked her knees to remain upright. She was too shocked to speak in her own defence, appalled at the unwitting part she was playing in the destruction of the creatures she loved so much.

Haveron's cold laugh startled her back to awareness. 'You know what really amazes me?' he asked contemptuously. 'That you actually used that poor doe as bait. If I hadn't seen it for myself, I wouldn't have thought you were capable of that. For God's sake, Jessie!'

His voice trembled for a moment, but became hard again with his next words. 'We worked for weeks to save that deer, and now you've put her on a wanted poster that will be circulated across the whole country. Why don't you just go out there and shoot her yourself?'

'No!' Jessie cried as moisture sprang to her eyes, and her lips tried to form the words of denial, but her mouth seemed to be frozen open in a small circle of shock. She kept seeing her paintings of Ice Cream, reduced and reproduced on the slick, glossy pages of a calendar; a calendar that would invite hunters from all over the country to come here to destroy the very creature whose trust had inspired the paintings. 'No,' she kept repeating dully, 'no, no, no.' Inside, her mind finished the denial, saying 'I didn't know, I never saw one of their calendars, I never even read their magazine, I didn't know.' But those words never reached her lips. They hung suspended in the silence of her jumbled thoughts, and Haveron never heard them.

If she had been aware enough to assess his expression, she might have noticed a faint glimmer of expectancy; that last vestige of hope which waited for her to make the very denial which was running through her mind. But all she could think of at that moment was the terribly irony of her situation; that her return to the only place she had ever called home was being financed by the very people who would destroy it. It had not yet occurred to her that Haveron would assume she had deceived him, used his trust to promote the violation of his sanctuary. When that thought finally tumbled into the numbing despair of her other thoughts, it was already too late.

'Wait,' she said breathlessly as he moved towards her and the door behind her. 'Wait. You don't understand. I have to explain. . .'

'Explain?' he asked sarcastically, lifting one brow. 'What's to explain? Your family has always made its living from hunters. You're just carrying on the tradition. I may have thought you had different standards, but that was my mistake, wasn't it? My mistake entirely.'

'Haveron . . .'

He flipped the hood of his parka up with a snap of his wrist and stared at her as she leaned against the door. 'Get out of my way,' he said levelly.

'No!' she cried. 'I will not! Not until you hear what I have to say! You can't just walk away from what we had without even listening!'

He stopped her protest with an incredulous, contemptuous smile. 'What we had? And what might that have been? A little physical diversion to while away an otherwise long, dull winter?' He raked her body unkindly with cold eyes, and Jessie's lips parted with dismay.

'No,' she whispered, shaking her head, denying his words. 'No. You can't mean that. . .'

'Oh, come now,' he smiled unpleasantly, 'surely you weren't naïve enough to believe it would be anything more than that?'

Oh, yes, she said to herself, her eyes wide and empty, her lips pressed tightly together. I believed it was more than that. A lot more.

His words fell like hard little stones on ears that barely heard them. 'I'll ask you once more,' he said. 'Get out of my way.'

And she did.

Jessie stood quietly, facing the door he had slammed behind him, feeling nothing for a moment but intense relief that he was gone, that the confrontation was over. She tried to organise her thoughts, to go over what had been said, to understand how everything right could so suddenly go terribly wrong; but it was too much to think about. The weight of the day's intense emotions was too heavy, and she simply couldn't carry it any more. Twice she had lowered the barriers long enough to accept Haveron, and twice he had been snatched from her at the last possible moment. The grief should have been terrible, but oddly enough, it wasn't. She could hardly feel it at all. All she felt was a strange distance from her own thoughts, as if her mind had been painted over with an opaque glaze.

She turned woodenly from the door and walked like a wind-up toy to the chair closest to the hearth; and there she sat, her mind as empty as the fireplace she stared at, while time passed in a grey succession of minutes she would never remember. She huddled there, in that safe, blank place the mind activates when retreat from the world becomes necesssary for survival, as the afternoon ticked slowly away.

Eventually, insidiously, the world crept back in; and one by one Jessie's senses clicked on again. My God, she thought, that's what it must have been like for Mother. That's what it's like when everyone else thinks you're going insane, and all you're really doing is going away.

She rubbed hard at her cheeks and shook her head until she saw spots of hot white before her eyes, hating herself for giving in to such weakness; but understanding for the very first time at least a fraction of what her mother must have felt twenty years ago, when her world had crumbled round her. She felt a rush of compassionate warmth for that gentle woman halfway across the country, and wished she could talk to her right now, if only for a moment. They'd kept in touch through the mails, with Jessie's abbreviated notes of reassurance always followed by long, chatty letters from her mother; but it wasn't the same as hearing her voice, and she decided she would call from Mr Ellis's store the moment the storm was passed.

As if answering her thoughts, the southwest windows rattled in a sudden gust, calling to her attention the wind that had been building steadily during the course of the afternoon. She glanced at her watch, frowned at the time that had passed, then closed her mind to everything but the essentials. She was wounded, but she wasn't dead, and a great deal remained to be done.

She went through the motions of bringing in the wood from the porch to stack by the hearth, making one tedious trip after another until her back ached and her palms were scraped raw by the rough bark. She was not consciously aware of any physical discomfort, and when she finally noticed a smear of blood on the last log, she opened her hand and looked with mild astonishment at the weeping wound on her palm, wondering where it had come from, and why it didn't hurt. She washed her hands briskly in the kitchen sink, absently noting the slight sting when water hit the raw skin. Then she gathered the dusty kerosene lamps from the back cupboard, trimmed the wicks, cleaned the chimneys, and finally filled them from the bottles that were stacked in one of the bags Haveron had brought in. Almost as an afterthought, she filled a bucket with grain, slipped on a jacket, and walked outside.

The wind hit her the moment she stepped off the porch, whipping her hair across her face in an icy blast that carried the sharp scent of coming snow. Jessie narrowed her eyes against it, oblivious to the sudden drop in temperature that was already making it dangerous to be outside.

She called into the wind as she rounded the cabin's corner, bent forward against the driving gusts; but there was no answering bleat, and the straw bed was empty. Her face crumpled as she knelt down and placed a gloveless hand in the straw where Ice Cream had obviously nestled for a time, but it was already cold to the touch.

Jessie stumbled round the cabin, her frantic calls snatched from her lips by the wind, searching vainly for some evidence of where the doe had gone. When the stiffness in her fingers became sharp pains of warning, she walked up on to the porch and stared into the thickening trees, hoping that Ice Cream had found her own safe harbour from the coming storm, and that she would not be alone, as she was.

The cabin door closed behind her just as the first

flakes of dry snow began to ride the wind, and she stood just inside for a moment, trying to catch her breath, totally drained by the cold.

Her heart ached with the loss of Ice Cream, compounding the loss of Haveron, yet her eyes remained strangely dry. Apparently, she thought, some pain goes beyond tears. Then her eyes dropped to the table that held the second bag Haveron had brought in. A thick, creamy liquid leaked from the bottom of the bag, oozing on to the smooth wood. Jessie unpacked the bread, milk and oranges from the top of the bag, then lifted out the last soggy parcel, dripping from one corner. It was a half-gallon carton of melting coffee ice cream.

Then she cried.

Jessie spent the rest of that evening doing things she would not be able to do later if the power went off as expected. She showered, washed her hair, and cranked up the cabin's electric heat until it was uncomfortably warm, reasoning that it would take that much longer for the cabin to cool down once her heat source was lost. She would not light a fire until it was absolutely necessary, both to conserve wood and because she knew an open flue would draw more heat in this wind than a fire could replace. Still, she was drawn to the cold hearth, and found herself sitting there in the yellow glow of lamplight while the ever-increasing winds battered the tiny cabin's walls.

Night had not crept softly into the forest this time; it had fallen like a crashing black blind. Only the light from the cabin windows reflected the snow that was now driven before the wind in a thick, flapping blanket. It fell at the rate of three inches an hour, and by ten o'clock, when the lamps in the living-room finally flickered once, twice, and then died altogether, the drifts on the cabin's west side were already climbing towards the eaves.

The howling wind seemed even louder, even more

sinister in the pitch black of the cabin, and Jessie's hand shook as she struck a match to light the kerosene lamp at her side. She went outside once more to search for Ice Cream, but came back into the cabin quickly, her lashes thick with frost, her lips drained of colour and her coat blanketed with snow. The doe had not returned.

Later, lying alone in the dark on her bed with the wind's haunting melody as background, Jessie finally allowed her thoughts to reach back tentatively and touch the pain of the afternoon.

She wanted to believe that Haveron had merely been striking back; that he had been so wounded by what he thought was her betrayal that he had simply lashed out, returning the hurt, blow for blow. But there was an ugly ring of truth to what he had said, and a terrible logic. Was it so unusual for men to pretend love to lure women to their beds? It happened all the time, didn't it? And after all, he had never actually said he loved her; he had never promised the lifetime she had assumed would be forthcoming. He had only promised the winter. In fact, those were his precise words: 'We have time,' he'd said. 'It's going to be a long, long winter.'

'Oh, God,' she moaned, pressing her face into her pillow. What an easy target she'd been! Completely inexperienced in the ways of men she'd spent years avoiding, she'd fallen for the very first line she'd heard. Naïve? Somehow that seemed an understatement of what she had been.

The deep, bitter anger of a fool's injured pride welled up inside her as she realised how very close she had come to being shabbily used. And then her face coloured with shame in the black of the darkened room, because whether or not he would have been using her, she knew she wanted him still.

Her last, agonised thoughts were of Ice Cream when the blessed relief of sleep finally came for her.

CHAPTER FOURTEEN

It was the cold that finally woke Jessie the next morning, creeping with icy fingers through the layers of blankets that covered her. She sat up in bed, her teeth literally chattering, clutching the covers around her. The daylight in the room seemed dull, somehow diffused; and a glance at the window explained the cause. The glass was solid white with snow, and from the inside looking out, Jessie could not tell if it had drifted that high during the night, or if it was simply a thin layer the wind had blown against the glass. She guessed from the silence that the worst of the storm was over, and cherished a faint hope that Ice Cream might be outside the cabin even now, waiting for her breakfast.

She shivered uncontrollably as she dressed in thermal underwear, heavy slacks and two loose-fitting sweaters worn on top of one another. Her face and her hands felt stiff and dry away from the relative warmth of her bed, and she guessed correctly that the cabin's temperature had dropped close to freezing point during the night.

A light dusting of snow had blown in around the frame of the kitchen window, and now lay unmelting on the wet counter, a bleak testament to how cold the cabin really was. Jessie brushed it impatiently into the sink with her bare hand, regretting the gesture immediately as her fingers prickled with cold.

Before thoughts of her own breakfast even occurred to her, she filled a bucket to the rim with grain, dressed carefully in arctic boots and parka, and went outside on to the front porch. She gasped at her first glance at the altered world around her, pulling frigid air painfully into her lungs.

There was no colour anywhere. Every tree trunk,

every stand of brush, every inch of ground was now layered with a thick blanket of snow so white it hurt her eyes to look at it. The wind had swept the porch clean of all but a fine layer of snow, but the cabin's west side was virtually buried under a mountainous drift that gave no indication that a small house sat beneath it. Jessie gaped at the spot where the bathroom window should be, and rejected thoughts of shovelling her way in to clear the glass just as soon as they crossed her mind. There would be no daylight in the bathroom for the rest of the winter, but at least the mound of snow would act as insulation from the cold and wind.

The east side of the cabin had been sheltered from the face of the storm, and was relatively bare. Only the recess of her bedroom window had caught the swirling snow and held it fast in a thick sheet of frozen white. She could chip that away later, but for now, her thoughts were concentrated on the snow-dusted bed of straw that still sat empty. Jessie's heart contracted with disappointment not to see the doe there, and she left the bucket near the cabin wall in case the doe should return.

The heavy layers of clothes she wore constricted her movements, and she walked with a stiff-legged gait back to the front porch, peering up to the roofline to make sure the chimney was not buried. For the first time she understood why the cabin's roof was angled so steeply, and why the chimney was so disproportionately tall.

She paused on the porch, staring off into the trees, still hoping senselessly that Ice Cream would come bounding from the tunnels of white at any moment, bleating for her breakfast. Finally she sighed and went back inside.

It took all day for the fire to bring the cabin temperature up to a tolerable level. Jessie kept the blaze hot and high, frowning at the rate the hungry flames consumed her dwindling stock of wood. She cooked soup and boiled coffee on a small grate that squatted over hot coals on one side of the large fireplace, ever conscious that her body would require continuous warm feedings to combat the cold during her frequent, futile trips outside to look for the doe. At one point in late afternoon, the sun peeped feebly through the heavy cloudbank, scattering dazzling diamonds of light across the snow; but it was hidden again almost immediately as the thick clouds rolled on.

Jessie lit all the kerosene lamps at dusk in a feeble attempt to fill the living-room with light. All it really enabled her to see was how little wood she had left. There was enough to get her through the night, but no more. If the power did not come back on by morning, she would have to brave the weather to search for more deadwood. She shivered at the prospect, and thought longingly of the lodge with its emergency gasoline generator and oil furnace; but she knew she would not go to Haveron for help, no matter how desperate she became. Perhaps she had been a naïve fool, but she did not need the reminder of his amused contempt. Freezing was preferable.

She spent a restless night on the couch in front of the fireplace, waking every hour or so to pile on more wood. At five o'clock she gave up the effort of sleep altogether, in spite of an aching body that cried out for uninterrupted rest.

She stumbled through the dim light cast by the fire's glow, relighting all the lamps, then scooped snow from the porch in a metal bucket that she set on the hearth. When the snow had melted and the biting chill was gone from the water, she washed and brushed her teeth as best she could in the bathroom, squinting at her reflection by the feeble glow of a kerosene lamp. Even making allowances for the shadowy lighting, she still looked like someone battling the ravages of a long-term illness. Her face was pale and drawn with fatigue, and dark smudges under each eye stood out against the pallor of her complexion. She brushed furiously at her hair as if that would improve her overall appearance, but even the smooth fall of brown looked dull and lifeless. She held her eyes half-closed to soothe the membranes irritated by dry air and woodsmoke, and when she opened them wide she could see tiny veins of red tracking through the whites.

'Beautiful,' she muttered, slamming her hairbrush down on the sink.

She forced her aching body to go through the motions of dressing, feeding the fire, and putting coffee on to boil. By the time she had forced down the bowl of oatmeal she knew she needed, it was light enough to turn down the wicks on all the smelly lamps.

It was still too cold in the cabin to draw, and Jessie stared disconsolately at her sketchbook, knowing her fingers needed to be warm and nimble to make use of it. It was just as well, really. Somehow her art had always been an expression of joy, no matter how deeply the joy was buried inside her; but now there was none at all to transfer to canvas, and she wondered if she would ever paint again. She stared at her idle hands with a wry smile, remembering all the years she had wished for time alone to paint, to read, or simply to cherish the privacy. Perhaps, if that opportunity had come before Haveron, she would have enjoyed it; but now, solitude seemed a very cruel sentence. She had no heart to sketch or to read, and so she was condemned to the endless litany of thoughts that all began with the words 'if only'.

She almost looked forward to gathering wood, even though she knew it would be exhausting, back-breaking labour. At least the physical exertion would divert her thoughts for a time, so she dressed in several layers of warm clothing and went outside.

The bright, winter-blue sky made a striking contrast to the world of blinding white, and Jessie had to go back inside to find the tinted goggles that would spare her eyes from the brilliant glare of sunlight bouncing off snow.

The still-full grain bucket sat untouched, just as she had known it would be, and she stood quietly for a while, staring at it, feeling more alone than she ever had in her life. Lack of motion intensified the cold after just a few moments, and she forced herself to begin digging through the snow-covered brush close to the cabin, searching for usable wood. Within an hour she had gathered enough to get her through the day, but she had exhausted the resources close to the cabin, and knew she would have to go into the woods to find more. She considered taking a short break in the cabin's relative warmth, but decided to make one short trip into the trees before claiming rest as a reward. She had gone no more than a few dozen yards into the trees when she saw something that made her stop abruptly, her heart pounding. There in the snow before her was an irregular splotch of pink, more intensely coloured in the centre, bleeding to paler and paler shades as the edges wept into the white fluff. She could barely make out the tiny, pointed prints of deer hooves moving away from the pink, and, following them cautiously, she came upon another patch of pink, and then another, appearing every so often along the deer's trail. She opened her mouth to scream Ice Cream's name, but then she saw the other prints, and her jaw closed with an audible click. They were large, waffled boot tracks, etched deeply into the snow by the weight of a heavy man, obliterating the prints of the deer he tracked.

Jessie stopped suddenly, her eyes wide, torn between her fear for Ice Cream and her fear of a hunter so avid that he would risk posted land, heavy snow, and bitter cold in his thirst for the kill. She agonised over her limited options, every muscle tensed, waiting for her mind's command. Finally she realised that she had never really had any options at all. Alone, she was powerless either to help a wounded deer or to face a wary poacher. She had no choice. She had to get Haveron.

She turned and began to run, lifting her knees high to clear the snow where it had drifted between the trees. Out of breath and exhausted by the time she reached the cabin's small clearing, she realised that running was out of the question on the relatively open trail to the lodge. The trees stood just far enough apart to allow the heaviest accumulation of snow there, and she stood staring at the smooth, unbroken sheet of white, well above her knees. Fortunately it had not yet settled into an impassable hardpack, and she pushed doggedly forward through the dry fluff, literally ploughing a path with her legs. Her boots filled with snow within a matter of minutes, but she didn't notice the cold dampness seeping through her heavy woollen socks. All she could think of was her last panicked run to the lodge, while Ice Cream lay wounded at the cabin. Haveron had been the saviour then, and he could be again, if only she could reach him in time.

She pushed harder, faster, through the deep snow, panting with the effort, flipping the parka hood back off her perspiring forehead. At the top of the ridge she paused for breath, her chest heaving, her throat dry and sore, remembering the last time Haveron had gone out to track a poacher and a wounded deer. She began to shake uncontrollably, remembering the deadly chill in his eyes and the frightening rage he had kept barely in check; and then suddenly it didn't matter. She could face that, she could even face his contempt for her, as long as there was still a chance to save Ice Cream.

She ran the last few steps up to the porch, lifting her feet high to clear the snow; then she stumbled up the stairs and burst through the lodge door without pausing to knock.

'Ice Cream,' she gasped as Haveron came running to the entry-way in response to her desperate call, '. . . blood. . .deer prints. . .and boot tracks near the cabin. . .' she could barely find the breath to speak, '. . . and she's been gone since the night of the storm. . .' Then she sagged against the door as the frost from her lashes melted and ran down her cheeks like tears.

He just stood there, staring at her, his hands half-extended as if to catch her if she fell.

'Oh, for God's sake, Haveron!' she gasped. 'Don't look at me like that! We don't have time! He's going to kill her!' She almost shrieked the last words.

He nodded once, then bent quickly and began to pull at one of her boots.

'What are you doing? There's no time for that . . .'

He jerked off one boot, then quickly removed the other. 'Now go in by the fire,' he ordered, 'and take off all your clothes, right down to the skin.'

'What? Are you crazy?' she asked weakly.

'Do it!' he shouted, then he closed his eyes briefly and lowered his voice. 'Look at yourself, Jess!' he whispered intensely. 'You're soaked through. You can't go out like that, and I don't have time to argue with you. Now get out of those clothes, and I'll bring you down some dry ones. Now hurry.'

Then he was vaulting up the steps three at a time towards the upstairs bedrooms, and Jessie moved stiffly towards the fire in the main room, pulling off her damp clothes as she went.

Her slacks were snow-crusted and heavy with moisture that had already soaked through her long johns, and Jessie began to shiver as she pulled the clinging wet clothes from her body.

'Here.' Haveron was beside her suddenly, rubbing vigorously at her bare legs with a soft towel, his brows furrowed in concentration, his dark hair bouncing with his motions. He straightened and pulled her sweaters carefully over her head, then massaged her back and arms and shoulders quickly with the towel, but gently, as if she were a child. Within seconds the fire and the rub down combined to bring the pink warmth of renewed circulation back to her skin.

'Is your underwear dry?' He glanced cursorily at her thin bra and panties and she nodded mutely. 'Good. Put these clothes on—all of them. I'll be right back.'

There had been nothing intimate in the way he had handled her body; only a touching gentleness that made her feel cherished. His voice and his eyes had been efficiently businesslike, but his hands had been caring, and it made her heart ache.

'Ready?' He was back before she had finished dressing in the strange collection of too-large clothes, and helped her to step into a bulky, one-piece snowmobile suit.

'I won't be able to run in this,' she said, hurriedly rolling up the legs of the suit to stuff into the boots he set down before her.

'You won't have to. Here. Put on the rest.'

Within five minutes of when she had first stumbled into the lodge, they were both dressed in snowmobile suits, gloves, and ski masks that covered all but their eyes and mouths. Haveron looked alien and sinister in black from head to foot, and if anything the one-piece suit accentuated the lean grace of his body. Jessie felt like a clumsy red blob in the too-large suit as she staggered towards the front door, and wondered what possible help she could be when her movements were so restricted.

Haveron paused at the door to snatch a rifle leaning barrel-up against the wall, and slipped the strap over his shoulder.

'Haveron, please don't . . .'

She could see only his eyes through the cut-outs in his black ski mask, but they seemed calm, and sad.

'We may need it for the deer, Jessie,' he said quietly, and she closed her eyes in resigned understanding.

Once outside they tramped round the side of the lodge to the garage and mounted the huge, black snowmobile that sat there, both wincing at the sudden, ear-splitting roar of its engine. Jessie clung tightly to Haveron's waist as they flew over the trail to the cabin in a fraction of the time it had taken Jessie to walk the distance; then she directed him with gestures to the break in the trees that marked where she had found the tracks.

Haveron guided the noisy machine carefully through the trees, nodding when she pointed to the first pink stain and set of tracks; then following them on an erratic course as they zig-zagged through a frozen swamp and a tight stand of cedar, before breaking out on to the main trail that led from the highway to the lodge. He turned off the machine and dismounted there, and Jessie's ears rang in the sudden silence. He stripped off one glove and knelt to examine the splotch in the snow that was a brighter pink than any of those previous. Then he rose to his feet, peeled off his mask, and stared down at her as she sat on the machine.

'We're getting closer. This one isn't frozen solid yet. It's going to be footwork from here on in, or the snowmobile will scare them both off.' He nodded at the tiny deer prints, and the large, menacing boot tracks that followed. 'This is as far as you go, Jessie.'

She was about to protest when a distant, clattering sound made them lift their heads in unison and stare off towards the highway. Four snowmobiles approached with a deafening roar, their riders dressed in suits and helmets with full-face, darkened visors, looking like huge, avenging insects from some nightmare.

The machines stopped just a few feet from where they waited, both standing now, and the riders turned off their engines. The largest dismounted and pushed back the sunscreen visor, revealing a white grin through the frost of his dark blond beard.

'Toby!' Jessie cried, peeling off her mask.

'Jessie! Boy, am I glad to see you!'

Then the other three removed their helmets and Jessie recognised Don Peltier, Elmer Harton and old Mr Ellis; the same men who had greeted her that first day at the store.

'We thought we'd better check up on you, Jessie,' Mr Ellis said kindly. 'What with the storm and all. They tell us we might not have power for a few days yet, and we were afraid it might have caught you by surprise.'

Jessie's glance took in the bulging saddlebags on each machine, stuffed with canned goods, and had to swallow hard. How do you thank people for a thoughtfulness that comes naturally when you're all forced to band together against the elements? She gave up trying and simply smiled with a helpless shrug. The gesture was so awkwardly comical in the huge suit that all the men laughed. Except Haveron.

Jessie caught his dark suspicious gaze at the men, and felt the spark of mutual hostility between them; for all of these men, with the exception of Toby, were hunters, or men who made their living from hunters.

Smiles faded, and the silence became ponderous. It was Mr Ellis who finally broke it. 'Well, I can see that you're in good hands here. Nobody knows these woods like Haveron. We'll just drop this stuff off at the cabin, and you two can go on with your ride. Beautiful day for it, isn't it? Though I don't recall that you ever liked snowmobiling much as a sport.' He levelled a questioning stare of Haveron, who said nothing.

'We're tracking a wounded deer,' Jessie blurted out, cringing under Haveron's sharp glare that clearly commanded her silence. 'And a poacher.'

There was a mumbled undercurrent from the men, and they all stiffened on their machines, seeming suddenly taller.

'That so?' said Peltier, whose eyes reflected an intensity Jessie could not read.

'A poacher?' Toby asked. 'In this cold, and all this snow? Again?' He had already told the other men about the doe Jessie and Haveron had saved.

Jessie pointed silently at the pink patch in the snow and the heavy boot tracks next to it, and the men were quick to dismount and follow the trail a few paces into the woods, where they conferred quietly with one another.

'Bastard!' Elmer Harton hissed as they all returned to their machines. Haveron stiffened, nearly purple with rage, assuming the comment was directed at him. He glared at Harton as the older man approached him, and Jessie could feel the tension about to explode. Then Harton spoke again.

'Well, come on, Haveron. You'll have a hard time bringing him in alone, whoever he is. Let's go.'

The other men lined up in a row, looking quietly at Haveron, waiting for him to lead the way.

Haveron just stood there, his eyes darting suspiciously from one face to another. 'This isn't your problem,' he said stiffly. 'I can handle it myself.'

'The hell it isn't,' Peltier said angrily. 'Poaching is everybody's problem, whether it happens on your land or someone else's. Now let's go get him, before he gets away.'

Haveron's features relaxed slowly, sagging into an expression of wary disbelief. 'You want to help me bring in a poacher?' he asked suspiciously.

'Listen, boy.' Mr Ellis put a hand on Haveron's arm. 'We may not see eye to eye with you in some things. You hate hunting, and most of us hunt. But that doesn't make any of us monsters—not you, and not us either. The real monster is out there.' He jerked his head towards the woods. 'Huntin' legal is one thing. Poachin' on posted land, that's something else. Especially when it happens more than once. Looks like this guy is going to winter here, unless we stop him here and now.'

Haveron dropped his head in a posture of confused uncertainty, and suddenly Jessie saw in him once again the embittered young boy, afraid to trust; and her anger at the man receded. But the eyes he finally lifted to look at her were still cold and indifferent, reminding her of his contempt. 'You can go back to your cabin now,' he said flatly, and she felt the pointed exclusion he had intended. I don't need you anymore, he seemed to be saying, and she stiffened defiantly at the implied rebuff. He was becoming a master at discarding her as soon as she had outlived her usefulness.

'No,' she said sharply, glaring at him. Not this time, Haveron, she thought to herself. Whether you have a use for me or not, I have a place here. For a little while longer; I have a place here, and I will not be cast aside. 'I'll wait at the lodge,' she said firmly. 'I want to know what happens.'

He stared at her for a moment, his brows lifted; then he simply nodded once and turned away.

CHAPTER FIFTEEN

JESSIE walked slowly back to the lodge, passing her cabin on the way, finding the going easier when she reached the trail she had broken earlier. She had refused Toby's offer of a ride back on his snowmobile, not wanting their pursuit of the deer and poacher to be delayed, and had offered a brave little smile when he'd told her she would have to learn to operate one of the machines herself soon. That was the kind of knowledge she wouldn't have much need for in Los Angeles.

She wasn't sure exactly when she had decided to go back, but at least the decision was made. She couldn't possibly go through with the calendar contract now, knowing to what use her paintings would be put. She would have to borrow money from Walt to pay back the advance, and, distasteful as that prospect was, it would be better than having her work used as an invitation to hunt its subjects.

She savoured the long walk through the snow-hushed tunnel of trees, knowing it would be one of her last; heartsick that she would have to leave so soon the place she had waited so many years to see again. But without the calendar money she had no means of support, and living in Haveron's shadow for an entire year would have been unbearable anyway.

When she finally reached the lodge, she turned on the porch to look out over the forest she loved. At that moment the stillness was broken by the sharp crack of a rifle shot, and Jessie jumped, holding her breath, but there was no further sound. They had found the deer, then, and she had been too severely wounded to save. She felt a hand tighten into a fist around her heart, but already she was relearning that sad process of keeping all the pain inside. She turned sadly for the lodge door, saving her grief for later, and went in to make coffee for the men. Somehow she knew they would all come back together.

She went back out on to the porch when she heard the snowmobiles roar up to the lodge. She stood there, a tiny, forlorn figure in Haveron's baggy clothes, her dark eyes quiet, hugging herself against the cold.

Haveron was up the steps first, his face tight and closed and expressionless.

'She's dead, isn't she?' Jessie asked tonelessly.

He looked at her, nodding, and perhaps it was the very lack of caring in her face that made him realise what she was thinking. 'No, Jess,' he said quickly, 'It wasn't Ice Cream. It was another doe.'

She said absolutely nothing. She simply closed her eyes, and held them closed.

'Get inside,' he said gruffly, turning her towards the door with a rough hand on her shoulder. Then he waved one arm to welcome the other men into the lodge, and soon they were all sitting around the fire, drinking hot coffee Haveron had laced generously with brandy, wolfing down sandwiches Jessie had prepared.

'Imagine him coming back,' Mr Ellis mused, finally leaning back in his chair and patting his stomach. 'Scares you, sometimes, to think how many armed men with a grudge there must be in the world.'

'Who came back?' Jessie asked. Up to now she had been patient, waiting for the men to eat and drink and warm themselves before asking what had happened in the woods; but she'd found Haveron's eyes on her more than once, and now she was almost desperate to hear the story and then escape to the solitude of her cabin.

'The man I shot in the foot last year,' Haveron said, watching her carefully. 'I had a sick feeling then that he wasn't going to leave it alone.'

Jessie sighed with relief when Toby took over the conversation. It gave her an excuse to look away from the cold light in Haveron's eyes.

'Mr Bart Masters himself,' Toby said, shaking his

head a little in disbelief. 'He was out to kill every single deer on this land, just to get back at Haveron.' Toby kept shaking his head, but Mr Ellis saw the flare of concern in Jessie's eyes.

'I wouldn't worry about him coming back, Jessie,' he said kindly. 'Michigan doesn't take kindly to illegal hunting. He'll lose his guns for sure, but besides that, I don't think he'll be too anxious to set foot on this property again anyway.'

The other men exchanged sheepish grins, but Jessie only frowned. 'And why not?' she demanded. 'He can buy other guns. What's to stop him?'

'Fear,' Mr Ellis answered with a smile. 'That . . . and gratitude.'

The other men burst out laughing, and even Haveron forced a reluctant smile. Jessie jumped up from her chair, her hands tightened into fists at her sides. 'It isn't funny!' she shouted. 'The man obviously wanted revenge, and he might still come back to get it, no matter what you threatened to do!'

Toby held up his hand and controlled his laughter with effort. '*We* didn't threaten him, Jessie. When we finally found the guy, he was halfway up a cedar tree screaming bloody murder for someone to save him.'

'Save him?' she asked in confusion.

'From our friend the black bear, Jess,' Haveron said quietly, and she turned to find his eyes as surprisingly gentle as his voice had been. 'They don't hibernate straight through the winter, you know. They come out of their dens every now and then, just to look around, and when they do, they're usually pretty bad-tempered.'

Jessie's mouth dropped into a circle as she remembered her lonely walk back to the lodge, and Haveron shook his head as if he could read her thoughts. 'The bear didn't really mean any harm. He was just curious, and a little irritated at all the noise Masters was making.'

Mr Ellis cackled with glee and slapped his knee. 'That ole bear treed him like a coon, didn't he?'

'But Haveron was the real topper,' Don Peltier put in, chuckling. 'He walked right up to that tree and said, real serious-like, "Don't move, Masters. That bear has attacked before, and you've made him mad enough. I'll try to lure him away."'

The men burst into laughter again.

'*Has* he attacked before?' Jessie whispered fearfully.

'Of course not,' Haveron answered. 'He was just cranky, whining like any other tired kid who wanted to go back to bed. It's just that when a bear whines it usually sounds pretty ferocious, but it was easy to chase him away.'

'But Masters didn't know that,' Toby smiled. 'He thinks Haveron saved his life, and came down that tree promising never to come back here again, swearing he'd turn himself in for poaching the minute he got back to town.'

'I'll bet he won't,' Jessie said sullenly, thinking of the wounded doe fleeing through the woods in pain and fear until Haveron's bullet brought her to a merciful end.

'He will, Jess,' Mr Ellis said kindly. 'We took his wallet, for one thing, and told him the law would go a lot harder on him if they had to track him down at home.'

Haveron made the rounds of the small circle and refilled all the mugs with fresh coffee and more brandy, stopping last in front of Jessie. She covered her mug with her hand, refusing to look up at him, even though he remained standing there, waiting for her attention. The moment dragged on, attracting a few curious glances. 'No, thank you,' Jessie finally said, still refusing to look at him. He hesitated for a moment longer, then returned to his chair. Jessie glanced up, past Haveron, to find Toby's eyes on her in a silent question. She forced a small smile, staring at that kind, open face, wondering why she couldn't have fallen in love with him, if she had to do it at all. Toby returned her smile and nodded, as if agreeing with her silent thoughts, then turned to look directly at Haveron.

'Too bad about the doe,' he said. 'She had a bad time.'

Haveron glanced at Toby with a brief, distracted smile, as if his thoughts had been elsewhere, then turned back to a morose contemplation of the fire. Jessie had an unobstructed view of his profile from this angle, and felt free to study him as long as she didn't have to meet his eyes. She wondered what he was thinking as an awkward silence filled the room.

He wore the dark, driven look of a man trapped by his own self-imposed solitude. He had never belonged in the company of others, and removed himself from it now simply by the way he sat, sipping quietly from his mug, lost in his own silence. He might as well have been sitting in the room alone. The other men sensed his distance, and began to fidget uncomfortably in their seats, looking round the large room with pretended nonchalance, searching for some point of interest that might start a conversation. Only Mr Ellis seemed totally at ease, watching Haveron with undisguised interest that went unnoticed.

'The lodge looks mighty fine,' he said finally, blue eyes twinkling in a net of wrinkles. 'Almost like it used to, just before opening day, wouldn't you say?' He looked directly at Haveron.

'Almost,' Haveron answered without thinking; then he stilled suddenly, his mug suspended at his lips, his eyes jerking towards the old man.

Jessie caught her breath, waiting for someone to ask how Haveron could possibly know what the lodge had looked like in its heyday, but the question never came. Apparently the other men had missed the underlying point of Mr Ellis's question.

The old man simply smiled at Haveron and nodded, content to have his suspicions confirmed. It was the story Toby told about the wounded doe that had started him thinking, remembering the sullen boy who had lived here before, a boy who would be Haveron's age by now. He had chided himself when he finally made the connection for not seeing it right away; but it troubled him a bit, not knowing why the boy had come back as a man. His smile broadened into a sheepish grin as Haveron stared at him suspiciously. He felt just a little guilty for tricking the man into revealing himself that way, but he didn't think any real harm could ever come from the truth. Besides, he was probably the only one left in these parts who could really remember Ron Michels, and all the trouble he'd made with the hunters back in those days. Except for Jessie, of course. His old eyes sharpened suddenly and shifted to Jessie as he wondered if she knew.

Jessie's worry was written all over her face. Haveron already disliked her enough without thinking she'd told Mr Ellis who he really was. Even now his gaze was on her, measuring, trying to decide if she'd betrayed him again. Apparently Mr Ellis saw his suspicion, and understood the situation instantly.

'Amazing how much old men can remember, isn't it?' he asked Haveron amiably. 'Of course, you're never real sure your memory isn't playing tricks on you, so sometimes it's better to forget the things you remember.'

Haveron relaxed visibly and inclined his head towards the old man, as if acknowledging a point, then his gaze shifted to take in all the men, one by one. A tiny smile tugged at the corners of his mouth as he ran his hand back through the thickness of his hair and rose slowly from his chair. For just one moment, staring up at him, Jessie forgot how much he had hurt her and ached for the outcast boy she could still see in the tall, strong figure.

'I'd like you all to come with me,' he said quietly, turning towards the games room. 'I have something you should see.'

The men rose as one, anxious for any diversion that would banish the awkward feelings which hung over this room, but Jessie held back.

'If you'll excuse me, gentlemen, I think I'll be leaving now.'

'Jessie?' Mr Ellis turned with a puzzled expression. 'Don't you want to see what Haveron has to show us?'

'I've seen it already,' she said woodenly, 'and I really have a lot to do back at the cabin.'

'Now, now, enough of this,' Haveron broke in with a falsely hearty voice. 'Of course you'll stay, Jessie.' He walked over and put a hand on her back, pushing her unobtrusively but very firmly towards the games room door. 'You of all people should be interested in the next few moments.' She saw through his broad smile to the snide taunt beneath. 'After all, this is your childhood home. Aren't you just a little curious to know its future? It's about to be decided, you know.'

'It's future? What are you talking about?' Harton asked. 'What's going on here?'

'Haveron . . .' Jessie tried to take a step backward and ran into the brick wall of Haveron's hand.

He circled her upper arm with his other hand in a clasp that looked friendly, but was actually painfully tight. 'You see, gentlemen,' he said smoothly, 'Jessie's plans for this area and my plans for this area don't quite coincide; and this might very well be the moment of truth. If anyone should witness this,' he looked down at her with an unpleasant smile, 'it should certainly be Jessie.'

Toby frowned at Jessie's stricken expression and was at her side in a moment, pushing himself between Haveron and her, pretending friendly persuasion. 'Come on along, Jess. I'll give you a ride home when we're finished here.' His eyes met Haveron's in a brief challenge that escaped everyone but Jessie, and Haveron tightened his grip on her arm momentarily, then shrugged and dropped his hand.

Toby held her back as the others followed Haveron towards the games room. 'What's going on here, Jess?' he asked with a concerned frown. 'There's enough hostility between the two of you to blow the place up.'

'Oh, Toby,' she sighed, dropping her head, letting her shoulders sag. 'You must have known what kind of a calendar it would be. Why didn't you tell me?'

'You didn't know?' he asked in astomishment.

'Of course not!' she whispered. 'I thought that magazine was a nature journal.'

Toby nodded grimly, understanding at last. 'Oh, brother. You didn't know what you were doing, and when Haveron found out . . .'

'He exploded,' she said flatly.

He grabbed her by the shoulders and turned her to face him. 'What are you going to do now?'

'The only thing I can do. I'll back out of the contract, return the advance money, and go back to California.'

'Toby! Jessie!' Mr Ellis called from the games room.

Toby's hand on her arm stopped her as she turned to follow the others. 'Jess,' he whispered urgently, 'you can't go back there! You waited all your life to come home!'

She smiled sadly and placed one hand on his bearded cheek. 'I don't have any choice, Toby.'

'But what about Haveron? He'll understand about the calendar, once you explain it to him. What about your relationship with him?'

She looked steadily into the kind blue eyes. 'There is no relationship, Toby, and there never was. I let my imagination get carried away, that's all. So, you see, explaining wouldn't make any difference. There's nothing here for me.'

'Ah, Jess.' He pulled her into his arms and kissed the top of her head. 'You're not giving him a chance, or yourself. He's just angry now, that's all. You owe it to him to at least try to explain.'

'No, Toby!' she hissed. 'You don't understand! Please, just leave it alone.' Her eyes pleaded with him not to ask any more questions. It was embarrassing enough to admit to herself that Haveron had never really been interested in anything but a physical relationship, without having others know the truth.

'All right, Jess, all right,' he reassured her, pushing her gently in the direction of the games room. 'We'll leave it alone for now.'

Jessie had to bite down hard on her lower lip to keep from crying. She hadn't realised until this moment how very much she would miss Toby, and suddenly it seemed that she was leaving everything she loved behind in Michigan, for the second time in her life.

Haveron's eyes brushed both Toby and Jessie with cold curiosity as they entered the room together, then he turned pointedly away, towards the model on the pool table, and began to explain his plans in a flat, tired voice.

'Well, I'll be damned,' Mr Ellis said some time later, echoing the sentiments of all the men who had listened in astonished silence for the last fifteen minutes. 'I'll be damned,' he repeated, shaking his head at the small toy buildings and hills and trails. 'I never expected something like this.'

Jessie frowned uncertainly from her position a little to one side and apart from the others, not sure if that reaction was good or bad.

Don Peltier jerked his head towards the model with his brows lifted. 'How many employees, you figure?'

'Fifty,' Haveron answered. 'Half to maintain the lodge and the cabins, the others to take care of the trails, keep the lake stocked, act as guides, and so on.'

Peltier nodded silently.

'You'll have to get that bordering land declared a refuge,' Elmer Harton warned, a perpetual frown creasing his brow. 'It won't work otherwise.'

'I know that,' Haveron answered warily.

'And there'll be some folks up here who won't like that much,' Harton continued. 'They already think too much of the prime hunting land has been taken over by the state.'

'Like the Martin brothers,' Mr Ellis sighed. 'I can see them stamping down to the State legislature, waving their arms, screaming about their God-given right to hunt being taken away.'

'Them and a few others,' Elmer mused thoughtfully; 'but they aren't fools. Just stubborn. Besides, they'd be crazy to fight this. It'll bring this town alive again. Hell, there'll still be plenty of places to hunt. And maybe, with this, some of us can afford to stay here to enjoy it.'

Jessie saw the shadow of optimism cross Haveron's face.

'It couldn't come at a better time,' Toby said. 'The lumber company is laying off next month. A lot of the men who have lived here all their lives already got notice, and they're going to have to leave. There just won't be any jobs here.'

'There will be jobs,' Haveron said carefully. 'If they want them.'

'You won't bring in outsiders?' Mr Ellis asked.

'Not if I can find employees here.'

'You'll find them all right,' Elmer said suddenly, sticking out a beefy hand towards Haveron. 'And I'll be first in line.'

Haveron's lips twitched as he accepted the offered hand and shook it, then he jumped visibly when Don Peltier clapped him heartily on the shoulder.

'Well,' Mr Ellis said, cocking his head to look at Jessie. 'I must admit I'm surprised you aren't in favour of this, young lady.'

Jessie looked up with a guilty start, as if every man in the room were silently accusing her of treason. 'But I am, Mr Ellis,' she said quickly.

'Well, now. That just doesn't make a whole lot of sense. This plan of Haveron's here depends on keeping the hunters out, and your calendar will do a whole lot to bring them in.'

She sighed and looked down at her hands, clasped tightly in front of her waist.

'She won't be doing any paintings for that calendar,' Toby broke in suddenly, ignoring Jessie's hand on his arm. 'She's never even seen a copy of the magazine. If she'd known what the calendar really was, she'd never have agreed to do it in the first place.'

Jessie closed her eyes to Haveron's startled gaze, at

the look of sudden regret that was softening his expression. It didn't matter any more. It wouldn't change anything.

'Is that true, Jess?' he asked softly, and the tone of his voice was so intimate that she thought when she opened her eyes there would be only the two of them in the room.

'Of course it's true,' she said flatly, meeting his gaze fully for the first time all afternoon.

'They'll sue you,' he said quietly.

'They won't get much.'

Mr Ellis nodded, beaming. 'Well, then, that's settled, and now everybody's happy.'

Jessie almost burst out laughing.

'And that's about all the good news this old body can stand for one day,' Mr Ellis went on. 'You have trouble with those boys in the State government, Haveron, you just let us know. But now we ought to be going. You ready, Jess?'

Haveron spoke before she could open her mouth to say anything. 'I'll take her back,' he said firmly, and not a man in the room, even Toby, thought to contradict that tone.

Mr Ellis made a point of lingering at the front door a few moments after the others had gone outside, fussing unnecessarily with the strap on his helmet. Finally he gave up all effort of pretence and looked directly at Haveron. 'There are some good folks up here,' he said earnestly. 'Maybe this town can do better by you the second time around.'

'And maybe I can do better by the town,' Haveron replied softly.

Mr Ellis nodded, smiling; then he chucked Jessie fondly under the chin before both men went out to join the others. Jessie waved to all of them, pretending a cheeriness she did not feel, then closed the lodge door to keep out the cold while she waited for Haveron to come back in.

She paced back and forth in the entry-way, building a

raging anger. There was only one reason why Haveron would want her to stay after the others had gone: he still thought he could salvage his plans for a winter playmate if he only apologised.

'Ha!' she exclaimed to the empty foyer, already imagining his contrite apology, furious that he would think she could be so easily manipulated. Did he actually think they could go back to the way it was, now that she knew his true feelings? 'Ha!' she said again, wondering how he would respond when she reminded him that without the calendar income she would have no money to finance her time here. She decided that if he was desperate enough for a companion he would probably offer her money, and the possibility of that happening made her quiver with rage.

Eventually she heard the machines outside roar to life, followed by Haveron's heavy tread on the porch stairs.

He came in silently, closed the door behind him, then leaned back against it with his arms crossed over his chest. His hair lay across one brow, and he tossed it back with an impatient jerk of his head; then he levelled dark green eyes on Jessie. His expression was shadowed by the straight line of his lowered brows, but his facial muscles were drawn into a mask of tight control that seemed to harbour anger more than the contriteness she had expected. As if he had a right to be angry with her!

'Toby tells me you're leaving,' he said in an unmistakably accusatory tone.

'So?' she demanded, her chin thrust forward, her brown eyes flashing with the cold light of righteous indignation.

'Is it that easy, then, for you to simply walk away?' His voice was barely controlled.

'Whether it's easy or not is none of your business,' she snapped, spinning away and walking back into the main room.

'You want an apology,' he said matter-of-factly as he followed behind. 'You want me to say I'm sorry for misjudging you about the calendar. Very well. Consider it said.'

She closed her eyes briefly in despair, then lifted her chin and turned to face him. He was doing precisely what she had expected—trying to salvage his chance for a winter's worth of female companionship with a few simple words of regret. Did he really think she would forget the rest of what he had said? That she was nothing more than a diversion?

'You amaze me, Haveron,' she said dully. 'I knew the first time I saw you that you hadn't a trace of human feeling; and still, you amaze me.'

'Now what the hell is that supposed to mean?' he demanded. It was the first time she had ever heard him raise his voice, and now she saw the anger, slicing across his brow in a black frown that made her take an involuntary step backward.

'Nothing,' she said quickly, turning away from him to search for the clothes she had discarded earlier. 'It doesn't mean a thing. Now where did you put my clothes?'

It was suddenly very important to get out of the lodge, away from his presence. Even now, hating him for using her, despising his lack of feeling, she could still feel his power. Despicable as he was, standing there like some black-clad avenger, prepared to toy with her for as long as it suited his pleasure, she still found herself drawn to him by the same self-destructive force that makes a moth batter itself to death against a lighted window. Leave me alone, she wanted to say, but she knew the words would reveal too much, and so they stuck in her throat while she scanned the room desperately for her clothes.

'They're over there,' he said, watching her eyes, jerking his head towards the corner of the room. 'I tossed them out of sight before the others came in. I wasn't about to explain how a pile of your clothes came to be in my living-room. They wouldn't have believed the truth, anyway.'

'I see.' She pulled the soggy pile of clothes from behind a chair and examined them briefly. 'They're still wet. If you don't mind, I'll just carry these, and return your clothes later.'

'Jessie,' his voice came softly from right behind her, and she turned quickly, fighting to control the wounded feelings that threatened to bubble into tears at any moment.

'I want to leave now,' she said shortly, hoping her voice sounded as cold as she had intended. 'And I won't be needing a ride. I'm getting used to the walk.'

He looked startled for a moment, as if he had never really expected she would want to go, then his gaze steadied. 'That doesn't make much sense,' he said quietly. 'Why suffer at the cabin with no heat or light, when you know there's a place for you here?'

Her despair solidified into a quiet, hurt anger that deadened every other emotion. 'I'm sure there's a place for me here,' she said icily. 'A very cosy place, no doubt, right in your bed; but did it ever occur to you that I might not want it?'

He looked at her steadily. 'No. I never considered that.'

She almost gasped at his conceit.

'Who are you trying to kid?' he hissed, snatching at her wrist. 'That wasn't such a repulsive thought to you a few days ago.'

She jerked her hand away and glared at him, her hands curled into tight fists at her side, her whole body quivering. 'A few days ago things were very different!' she shouted.

'Oh? In what way?' he asked with maddening calm, sliding his hands into the front pocket of his jeans.

'I had a job, for one thing.'

'I see. And that's the only thing that was keeping you here? Your job?'

Her hair spun in a wide circle round her shoulders as she turned away from him.

'You wouldn't have to worry about money, you

know,' his voice came from behind her, and she let her eyes fall closed at the final blow. There it was, out in the open, as common and as insulting as any man's offer to any prostitute. The emotions hit her so hard and so fast that they defied expression; and even as she felt the sickening crumble of the feelings he had finally destroyed, her face remained remarkably composed as she turned back towards him.

'My God,' she said softly, shaking her head. 'I must admit I expected better than that. Some sort of build-up, just for appearances, you understand. I never expected you to be so . . . direct.'

He blinked once, slowly, then shrugged. 'I didn't think I had much to lose by getting right to the point.'

She nodded almost imperceptibly, and her reply was cold. 'You're right. My answer would have been the same no matter how you phrased the offer. What surprises me is that you had the gall to make it at all. What in God's name made you think I'd even consider it?'

His eyebrows shot up and his lips parted in a cruel smile. 'This,' he said scornfully, reaching out to grab her shoulders, jerking her against him in one swift motion, crushing her mouth under his. She struggled against him, battering his chest with her fists, twisting her head so that his mouth dragged across her cheek and down to the hollow of her neck.

'No,' she protested weakly, straining away from him, shaking her head violently, feeling the involuntary pulse of her lower body as it pressed against his. She gasped when she felt the gentle pressure of his teeth against her throat, then he pushed her slightly away from him, just far enough to look down into her eyes.

'You want this,' he said hoarsely. 'You'll never convince me that you don't.'

'No!' she cried sharply, escaping his hold with one mighty shove, backing quickly away. 'I don't want it! I don't want you! Why would I?'

He lifted his chin slightly and his eyes darkened, almost as if he had been slapped.

'Such a tough lady, aren't you?' he breathed, clenching his fists at his sides. 'Harder than anyone you know, man or woman, that's how you see yourself, isn't it? Looking down your nose all your life at others who weren't as strong, offended by what you thought was their weakness. That's what you thought of your mother all those years, wasn't it? You thought she was weak, didn't you?' He was shouting now, his face livid, and Jessie took another step backward, her eyes wide. 'Well, she wasn't weak!' he said venomously. 'She was a better, stronger person than you'll ever be, because she had the courage to love someone so much that it nearly killed her when she lost him, and that's a kind of courage that you'll never have!'

'You have no right to talk to me that way!' Jessie shouted, her voice trembling, her knuckles white as she clenched her fists. 'And I don't know what you're talking about anyway! Why do you know about love? You've hated all your life, and you're still doing it! The only things you've ever related to are dumb animals! You just couldn't make it with people, could you?'

She heard the strident echo of her words when she paused for breath, and gasped to realise that the shrill sounds had come from her.

His lips curled in an unpleasant smile as he reached out to brush her hot cheek with the back of his hand. She shuddered under his touch in spite of her anger, or perhaps because of it.

'Not quite true, Jessie,' he said viciously. 'I related to you, or have you forgotten?' His hand dropped to the rise of her breast beneath the too-large sweater, and although she knew the brazen touch was meant as an insult, her hand refused to knock his away. She just stood there, trembling, humiliated by his contempt, and by her inability to resist him.

'Ah, I see you do remember,' he drawled. 'Then perhaps you consider yourself one of the dumb animals I relate to. Is that it? Was I relating to an animal that night by the fire? A thoughtless creature who responds only to bodily instincts, with no emotion at all? That would explain a lot of things, wouldn't it?'

His hand cupped her breast boldly now, and she closed her eyes to the cruelty in his face, and closed her ears to the cruelty of his words, becoming the animal he claimed she was, responding only to his touch. Perhaps it was worth his contempt, she thought bitterly; just to be this close to him, just one more time.

He smiled coldly at her crumbling resistance and grabbed the back of her neck to pull her towards him. She could feel the urgent pressure of his hand against the back of her head, grinding her mouth against his, and when her eyes fell closed, she thought she would simply pretend that his touch was gentle and loving; she would pretend that his eyes had been soft and warm; and as she pretended, her mouth opened under his and her body came alive and he jerked back, gasping, as if he had been burned.

He held her from him by the shoulders as if she were an animal to be kept at bay, and she watched as he tried to catch his breath, his eyes suddenly uncertain. 'My God, you're a cold bitch,' he breathed bitterly, and then he released her.

'Me?' she laughed weakly, trying to cover her own ragged breathing. 'I'm cold? And what does that make you? A man who would pay me for my services like some common whore, without a single thought for my feelings?'

He had started to walk towards the fireplace, but now he stopped, turning slowly to look at her, his lips parted in astonishment. 'What the hell are you talking about?' he asked slowly.

'About your "offer"!' she spat contemptuously. 'Your offer to pay me to spend the winter!'

She closed her eyes and let her shoulders slump, realising the futility of the entire discussion. Nothing she said would change him, or the way he felt about her.

'I didn't offer to pay you, Jessie,' he said quietly,

intensely, and she opened her eyes slowly to look at him. 'I told you that you wouldn't have to worry about money.'

She lifted her shoulders in a weak shrug, past caring now. 'What's the difference?' she said flatly, turning to walk away.

'The difference was the intention,' he said quickly, and an almost desperate quality in his voice made her hesitate before she took a step. 'I meant that you wouldn't have to worry about money as my wife. I thought you understood that.'

'What?' she whispered, afraid to turn around, afraid to look at him.

'I was asking you to marry me, Jessie,' he whispered thickly. 'My God, I can't believe you thought it was anything else.'

She turned to face him now, her eyes glistening with unshed tears. 'But at the cabin, the day of the storm, you said I was just . . .'

'I know what I said. I was angry; I was hurt, lashing out. You must have known that, Jessie. You must have known how I felt about you. How could a few words spoken in anger make you doubt it?'

'You were very convincing,' she said in a small voice, and then he covered the space between them with two long strides and wrapped her in his arms, burying his face in her neck.

'Oh, God, Jessie,' he murmured, and she felt his body tremble against hers as she wrapped her arms around his neck. 'I love you.' And then he laughed a little against her neck. 'I've never said that to anyone, can you imagine? And now that I've said it once, I don't want to stop. I love you, I love you . . .'

Jessie held her breath as she pressed against him, teetering on the precipice of commitment, still clutching desperately at that one strand of memory which warned her there would be no turning back once she let go; that her heart, her mind, even her life would never be totally under her control again. She would be like her mother, like every other woman who had ever relinquished that precious centre of existence which depended on another for happiness. And then he pulled away to smile down at her, and she saw the love and the warmth flood out from the strange green eyes to wash over her; and for the first time in her life she understood that it would be worth the risk.

'And I love you,' she whispered against his lips, feeling a tremendous weight lift from her heart and her mind and her shoulders, even as she said the words.

He slipped one arm beneath her knees and swung her up against his chest, cradling her carefully against him; then he walked over to the fireplace and sank to his knees, still holding her in his lap. As she looked up into his eyes, Jessie felt a tiny prickle of uncertainty at the back of her mind.

'What is it?' he asked, smoothing the faint line between her brows with his fingertip.

'Ice Cream,' she said sadly. 'I can't stop worrying about her. Do you think she's all right?'

He sighed deeply and smiled down at her, shaking his head slightly. 'Yes, I think she's all right. It was just time for her to go, Jess. I warned you that that would happen one day. She never really belonged to us, you know.'

'I know,' she whispered sorrowfully. 'I just wasn't ready yet.'

He picked up a strand of her hair and smoothed it between his thumb and forefinger, following its line from the top of her head to where it curved over her breast, smiling when she shivered under his touch.

'You know, I've been thinking,' he said absently, sliding his hand beneath her sweater, up to rest idly on the bare skin of her ribcage. 'We could use your paintings of Ice Cream in the promotional advertising for this place—that is, if you're willing to sell the reproduction rights.'

She saw his hand beneath the sweater rise and fall with the suddenly increased tempo of her breathing. She looked up into the vibrant green of his eyes and felt her heart skip a beat.

'And then,' he continued, his gaze never wavering from hers as his hand travelled upwards to circle her breast tenderly, 'I could hire you to do a calendar for me, one that would promote all the resorts.'

'All?' she breathed, arching her back as his hand slid down to deftly unfasten her jeans.

'Candervas,' he said thickly, his eyes narrowing, 'this one, and the next one, in Vermont.'

'Vermont?' she asked weakly.

'Vermont,' he repeated, closing his eyes at last while his lips parted to draw in a sharp breath. 'That's where we'll go next. Maybe next spring.'

She slipped out of his lap and on to the floor, pulling him on top of her with her hands locked behind his head.

'Do you think you can leave your home again,' he whispered, 'so soon after you've found it?'

She laced her fingers into the thickness of his hair and pulled his mouth down to hers, catching his upper lip gently between her teeth, caressing it with her tongue, thrilling to the low moan that escaped from his mouth. 'I won't be leaving home, Haveron,' she murmured against his lips. 'Not if I'm with you. I'll be taking it with me.'

He let the full weight of his lower body ease down on to hers, and she emitted a tiny cry at the bold thrust of his passion, straining into him, pulling at his waist to draw him closer. Suddenly her clothes were unbearably constricting, and she pushed him away just enough to sit up quickly and peel off her sweater.

'I think I'm supposed to do that,' he murmured, sliding the strap of her bra down her arm, closing his mouth around the exposed breast, gasping when her back arched and she pushed into him, pressing against the back of his head with her hands.

'You can do it next time,' she whispered raggedly, closing her eyes against the impossibly erotic sensation of his tongue against her nipple, submitting gladly to the hands that pushed her down on to her back.

'By the way,' he breathed heavily, 'you never told me. Did you like the ice cream?'

'The ice cream?' she gasped in a voice she no longer recognised as her own. Her thoughts were spinning frantically, trying to make sense of his words while his hands coaxed her body into its own mindless frenzy. 'Oh, the ice cream,' she suddenly remembered.

But then there were no clothes between them, and she was staring wide-eyed up at a face tight with desire yet still touched by love, and she was about to tell him about the ice cream when she felt the first shuddering touch of a union she'd been waiting for all her life. Oh, hell, she thought in that last clear moment when her mind was her own. I'll tell him later. Then she closed her eyes and pulled him down by the shoulders with the mysterious smile of a woman who knows exactly what she's doing.

CHAPTER SIXTEEN

THE doe lifted her elegant head from the empty bucket, her ears pricked towards the hammering clatter approaching from over the ridge. She blinked once, polished brown eyes focused towards the sound's source, every muscle in her body tensed for flight. As the noisy black creature vaulted over the lip of the ridge, two smaller creatures clinging to its back, she sprang in a series of graceful leaps that carried her safely into the cover of the trees, and there she turned and froze, watching, listening. The low-slung black creature fell suddenly silent, and then the doe heard the familiar voices of the Man and the Woman. Her ears waggled in wary anticipation as she lifted her nose to scent the air.

She jumped back at the sharp crack of the cabin door closing, then inched forward in delicate, cautious steps, confused by the acrid stench of the unfamiliar beast's loathsome exhalation. She paused at the edge of the forest and stared at the snowmobile. It was silent now, and perfectly still. Perhaps it was dead.

She watched it for a very long time, leary of the sunlight glinting off its shiny black surface, looking like so many sinister eyes, patiently waiting for the opportunity to pounce. But then the smell of the beast dissipated into the crisp freshness of the air, and she took another cautious step forward. Truly, it must be dead, or she would still be able to smell its foul breath.

She made a tentative sound deep in her throat, but the beast did not respond. She moved further out into the clearing, more confident now, her stomach rumbling from the deprivation of the last few days. The ravine she had found deep in the woods had been warm, and relatively sheltered from the fury of the storm and the lingering cold. There had even been the fresh scent of others of her own kind there; but she had missed the grain and the hay, and the strangely satisfying touch of the Man and the Woman. The scent of her own kind had been intriguing, tugging gently at some deep, inner instinct; but the lure of the Woman and the Man and their food was stronger, at least for now.

She stepped delicately through the deep snow until she stood directly in front of the cabin steps, quivering with anticipation, her eyes focused on that part of the cabin from which the Woman always emerged whenever she was called. Then her nostrils flared and she blew a trumpet of breath from her mouth.

Inside the cabin, two heads lifted simultaneously, and two pairs of human eyes locked in a silent expression of shared joy. Neither figure moved, wondering if the sound had been real, and then Ice Cream bleated again, louder this time, her neck extended, her head lifted, her eyes closing with the forceful expulsion of air from deep within her chest.

There was an answering clatter from within the cabin walls that told the doe her call had been heard. She snorted once in satisfaction and stamped her front foot, extremely pleased with the wonderful sound she had made, even more pleased that it would have the expected results. She would have grain and hay and the soothing hands of these peculiar two-legged creatures for all the time that the rain fell white and soft and lay in thick piles on the ground. And then later, much later, when the white rain soaked into the forest floor and the succulent moss sprouted in green wedges round the swamp; she would hear the siren song of a waiting buck, and the Man and the Woman would fade into the recesses of her limited memory. It was then that she would respond to her own irresistible call of home.

But not just yet.

She had everything a woman could want… except love.

Locked into a loveless marriage, Danica Lindsay tried in vain to rekindle the spark of a lost romance. She turned for solace to Michael Buchanan, a gentle yet strong man, who showed her friendship.

But even as their souls became one, she knew she was honour-bound to obey the sanctity of her marriage, to stand by her husband's side while he stood trial for espionage even though her heart lay elsewhere.

WITHIN REACH
another powerful novel by
Barbara Delinsky,
author of Finger Prints.

Available from October 1986.
Price: £2.95. **WORLDWIDE**

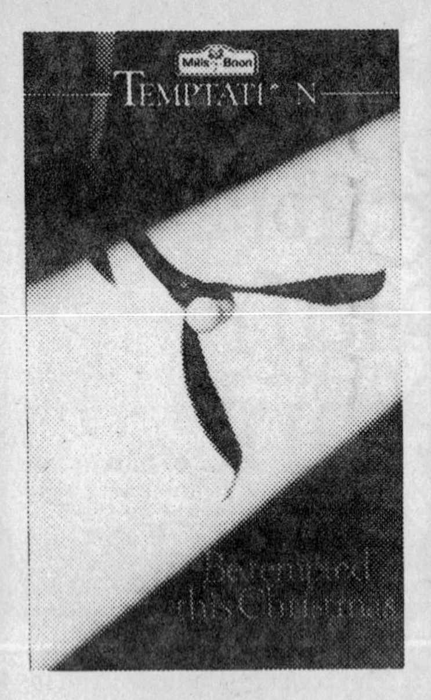

Merry Christmas one and all.

CHANCES ARE
Barbara Delinsky

ONE ON ONE
Jenna Lee Joyce

AN IMPRACTICAL PASSION
Vicki Lewis Thompson

A WEEK FROM FRIDAY
Georgia Bockoven

THE GIFT OF HAPPINESS
Amanda Carpenter

HAWK'S PREY
Carole Mortimer

TWO WEEKS TO REMEMBER
Betty Neels

YESTERDAY'S MIRROR
Sophie Weston

More choice for the Christmas stocking. Two special reading packs from Mills & Boon. Adding more than a touch of romance to the festive season.

AVAILABLE: OCTOBER, 1986 PACK PRICE: £4.80 Mills & Boon

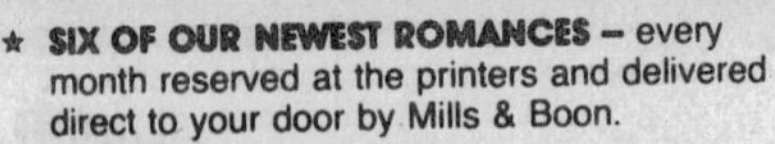

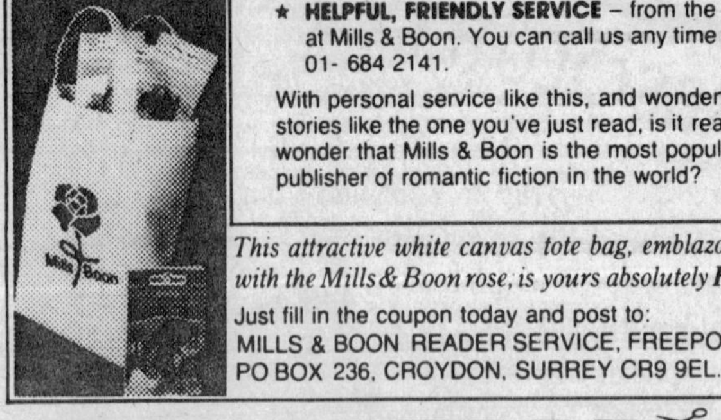
Mills & Boon

ASSOCIATION OF MAIL ORDER PUBLISHERS

mps